Holding you

JAMI ROGERS

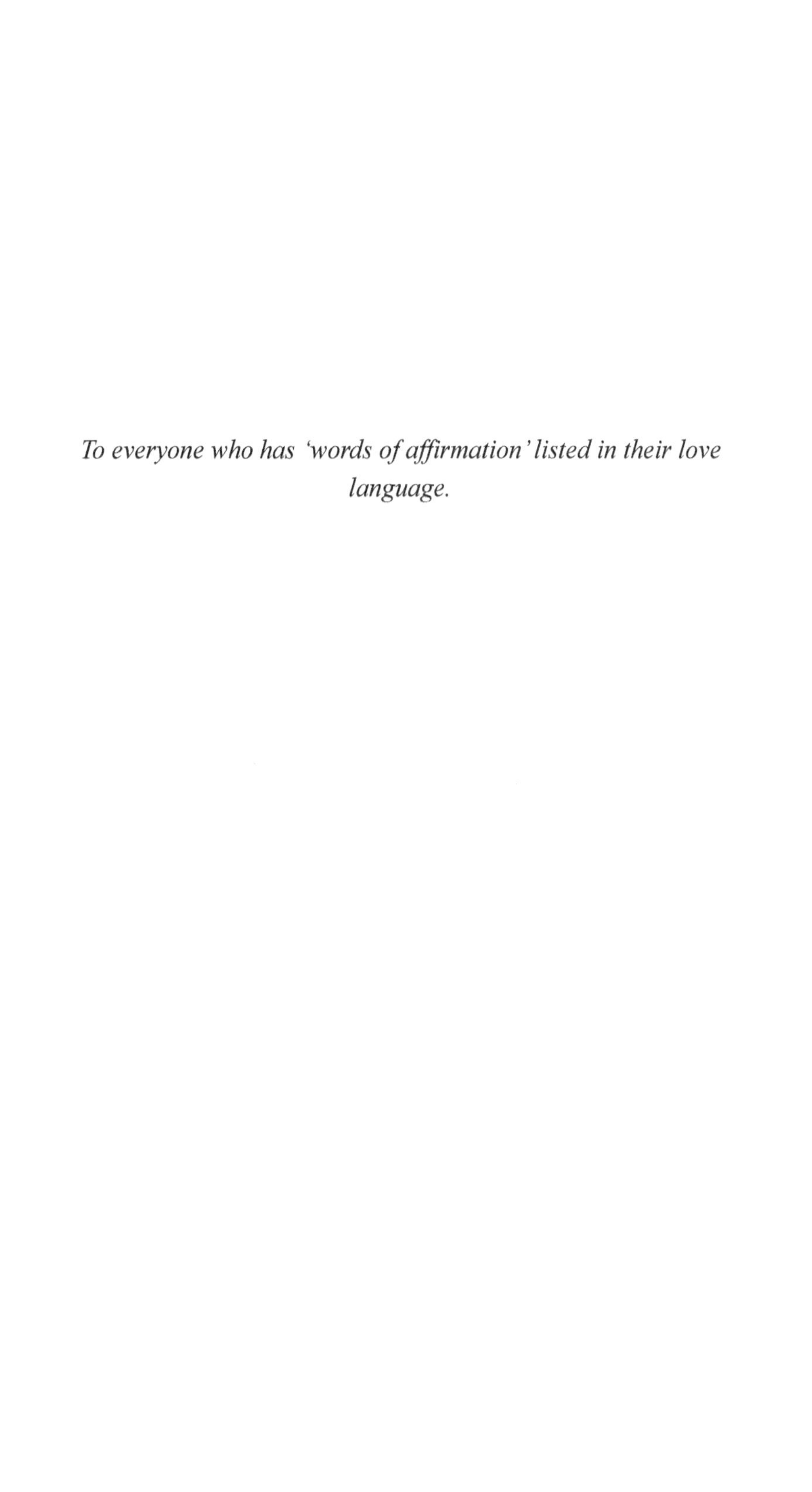

To everyone who has 'words of affirmation' listed in their love language.

HOLDING YOU
Copyright © 2025 by Jami Rogers
All rights reserved.

This is a work of fiction. Names, characters, businesses, places, events, and incidents are either the products of the author's imagination or used in a fictitious manner. Any resemblance to actual persons, living or dead, or actual events is purely coincidental.

www.authorjamirogers.com

Cover design © Hang Le byhangle.com
Editing by Julie Sturgeon, CEO Editor, ceoeditor.com
Proofreading by Emma Cook, Booktastic Blonde LLC

❀ Formatted with Vellum

Holding You

JAMI ROGERS

PROLOGUE

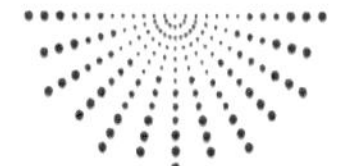

LAST SUMMER - DECLAN

There's nothing better than meeting your new neighbor, all because your daughter kicked a soccer ball so hard that it broke the fence you share with them.

We have been here for two days.

She didn't just crack it a little or put a small hole in it. No, she fully broke two boards and made a gap big enough that her body can fit through it. Given she's only eight, it doesn't have to be very big, but it's … big.

"Hi," I say with a wave as the back sliding door of the house next door opens. An older man pops out, looking up with a big smile as I jog across the yard to meet him.

"Declan Young. Is that you?"

I slow my steps, letting the older man fall into view. The sun is fading behind him, so I can make out his face.

"Paul Asher." I chuckle. "It's great to see you again," I say, stopping on my side of the fence, waiting for him to meet me.

He grins and points to the fence. "Is this your handiwork?"

"Yeah, my daughter was kicking her soccer ball around and

hit the fence. Any chance you can grab her ball and send it back over here?"

His back door opens again, and a little boy with dark hair appears. He looks at me with big chocolate brown eyes but glances away when our gazes meet.

He looks like he is about the same age as my daughter as he hides behind who I can only assume is his grandfather. But it's the little boy who spots the pink ball first.

He runs to it and without a second thought, pushes it through the fence.

It's at that moment I notice Susie, my daughter, behind me. She'd run inside to hide after she broke the fence, but I didn't see her sneak back outside.

"Thanks," she says softly.

"Did you kick that?" the boy asks.

"Yeah." Susie smiles.

Silence only lasts a split second before the boy asks, "Can I come play with you?"

Susie looks at me with wide eyes and a smile.

We've been back in Lovers for a couple of days now and haven't had a chance to make friends for her yet. So I can see right away that she wants me to say yes.

"Sure, if his parents say it's okay."

"Go for it," Paul says, and Max climbs through the fence to my yard.

Both kids begin to play as if they have known each other for years.

If only it were that easy for adults.

"I heard this place was for rent, but unfortunately, the rumor mill didn't provide me with much detail outside of that." Paul grins with a shrug.

I nod. "It happened pretty fast, so I gather there wasn't time to let the gossip spread."

"The town will be thrilled when they figure out that golden boy Declan Young is back."

I laugh.

My parents once told me that people here call me that. Just because I was smart doesn't mean I was perfect. I never understood it.

Born and raised in Lovers, I left to go to college. I'd always planned to come back, but then my parents moved away, and I met Susie's mom, and life happened.

It took me a lot longer than I planned to get back here, but I did it.

"The town will be just fine if they find out quietly."

Even as I say the words, I know they are pointless. This is Lovers. Gossip is basically a rite of passage here.

"Well, between you and Ruby moving back within the same week, I can only imagine what they will say."

"Ruby moved back. That's amazing. Is this her son?"

Paul beams as he nods. "Having them back has meant the world to me."

I don't know much about the story there, but I remember my parents talking about how hard it was on him when his daughter left.

Ruby Asher is younger than me. I went to school with her twin brothers and didn't really know much about her. Heck, her brothers and I were complete opposites, and even though we lived in a small town, we hardly spoke.

"She's actually moving into my house." He points at the one next to mine. "I'm downsizing into an apartment Miles built for me behind his shop."

"That's great." My eyes drift to where Susie is attempting to show Max a trick shot. He fails and lands on his butt, and the two of them erupt into laughter.

"Oh, here she is now," he says.

The patio door to his house slides open for a third time. A bare leg steps out. Next, it's an animal-print skirt that has a slit up the side, and from the way it flows, a pair of short, *short* black shorts underneath. Then my gaze falls to the simple white shirt that hugs her curves and displays a full chest.

I suck in a breath as her face comes into view.

Strawberry blonde hair frames her pink pretty lips, high cheekbones, and bright green eyes.

"Dad, have you seen Max?" she asks, clearly oblivious to the fact that the guy on the other side of the fence just spent a solid thirty seconds taking in every inch of her.

Wow.

Ruby Asher is nothing like I remember.

She's grown into a stunning woman, and I can't peel my eyes off her.

"He's playing soccer next door," Paul says and then he claps. "I think he made a friend."

"What? Really?" Ruby lights up and then rushes to the fence to peek over.

I'm hit with a floral scent, and my heart picks up.

It's been years since I've reacted like this to a woman.

I was beginning to think Susie's mom broke me.

But it seems maybe not.

"This is great. I've been worried about him making friends since we moved back." Ruby turns her attention to me, and a sweet, almost shy smile touches her lips.

Our eyes lock, and I swear she sucks in a breath.

"Hi," she says. "I'm Ruby."

"Ruby, hun, you know who this is, don't you?" her dad asks.

She blushes and shakes her head.

"No, should I?" Her tone is flirty as she looks at me for the answer.

I chuckle and am about to give her my name, but her dad beats me to it.

"It's Declan Young."

Now it's my turn to blush. He said my name like I'm important and she's supposed to be impressed by the name alone.

It's got to be a parent thing to do this to us.

"You're kidding," she says and the sweet innocent tone that laced her voice just seconds ago is gone, replaced with complete distaste. "Declan. Young."

I glance at her dad and then at her.

Ah, she's definitely not impressed by my name.

"That's … me," I say awkwardly.

She crosses her arms and pops her hip. I'd say it's cute, but I'm starting to get the feeling that she doesn't like me.

Which is crazy, because I can't think for the life of me of a moment where we interacted and it went badly.

"And you live *there*?" She points to my house.

I nod. "Yes."

"Since when? For how long?"

I let out a nervous laugh at the horror in her voice.

"We just came back and I'm not sure yet. A while, though."

"A while," she repeats.

"A while," I repeat, but this time with a little more snap.

Okay, her tone is starting to piss me off a little. You can't be rude to someone for no reason and expect them to just take it.

"Well, this is just great. I'm *thrilled* to have you next door."

I grin, crossing my arms and facing her. "You know, I'm just going to put this out there, but I don't think you mean that."

"Ha, you think?" She huffs and walks off. "Dad, bring Max home with you when you come inside, please."

Paul and I stand in silence until the door closes and Ruby is inside.

"Huh," he says first. "I get the feeling my daughter doesn't care for you very much."

I rub the back of my neck, watching the children again to clear my mind.

"Yeah … I caught on to that, too."

"Care to tell me why?"

His guess is as good as mine.

"If I knew, I'd tell you."

He laughs at that, and we fall into a conversation about how I landed back in Lovers and how much it hasn't changed over the years.

He can carry on a conversation, which is nice because all I can think about is how the woman next door doesn't like me.

And I have no idea why.

It bothers me.

"So yeah, you and your little girl should come to breakfast on Sunday. I won't take no for an answer."

"We'll be there," I tell him.

He calls Max in, and I lead Susie inside for dinner.

He might not take no for an answer, but I have a feeling I know who will have no problem giving him that answer, or me for that matter.

The one and only Ruby Asher.

CHAPTER ONE

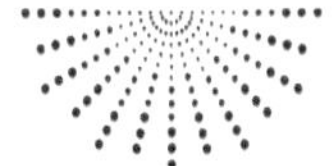

PRESENT DAY - RUBY

With a name like Ruby, most people assume you're named for having red hair.

But not me.

I got my name because, after having three boys, my mother finally got a little girl. The doctor told her all throughout her pregnancy it was a boy, but out popped me.

Apparently, she told my dad that I was a rare gem. Add in the fact that I was born in July, and they named me Ruby.

It's a total coincidence that my hair naturally settled on a strawberry blonde color.

I curl the last strand, wave my hand over it to cool it down before I spray it with hairspray, and then run my hand through all the curls to create a wavy style for the day.

Today is the last day at my son's elementary school. Living in a small town means everyone will find an excuse to celebrate and I mean *anything*.

Hence, it's today's last blast celebration for all the children and they are having a full-blown party with games and food in the parking lot.

Which means if I'm not out of my front door within the next sixty seconds, I'm going to be late.

I grab the tray of Funfetti cupcakes I baked this morning and frosted with white icing off the kitchen marble countertop. The dishwasher still needs to be emptied and the dishes in the sink need to be placed inside it. Then, I nearly trip over Max's shoes by the front door.

I'll just go ahead and add clean the kitchen and living room to the list of things that need to be done around the house, and keep my eyes off the grass that clearly needs to be mowed in the front yard.

I got this, though.

The point of moving back to Lovers last year was to take back control of my life. Sure, the life I was living before was easy, but it wasn't mine, and those who controlled it made sure I knew that every single day I was there.

Living near the elementary school has been a perk in my constantly crazy, busy life.

I turn right at the end of my driveway, glancing at the house next door as I walk by.

Growing up, the Stonewalls lived there. Their kids were older than me and my brothers, so I never interacted with them much, but Mrs. Stonewall was the sweetest after my mother died. I was really young when it happened. Oddly enough, I was the exact age of my son right now.

Eight.

I let out a sigh and pick up the pace.

Sweet ole Mrs. Stonewall doesn't live there anymore.

Instead, her son is renting the house out to Declan Young.

I wrinkle my nose as flashbacks of growing up and going to school in our small town hit me.

Oh, Ruby, dear, your score was one of the highest. Right under Declan Young.

Lovely, just lovely, Ruby. Your art piece has the second-highest student votes ever. Right after Declan Young.

Just one more point and you would have tied the school record with Declan Young.

Ruby Asher almost knocked Delcan Young out of first place for the school record in the mile.

I roll my eyes at no one. I was always second-best to the town's golden boy.

By default, this made me despise Declan.

It didn't matter that he was old enough that we were never in the same school at the same time.

Teachers and staff loved to bring up his name anytime they could.

Now, he owns one of the biggest anti-virus software companies in the world and our town is *still* talking about him.

Until my father invited him to Sunday breakfast and all three of my brothers decided to befriend the enemy last summer, I'd never really spoken to him, so, sure, I probably shouldn't care about this anymore.

But I do because this town has made it impossible to move on.

I'm twenty-five now.

It's annoying.

"Ruby!" One of the PTA moms, Sandy, calls me over as I reach the parking lot where the last blast games are being held.

I smile, thankful that the people of Lovers welcomed me back after so many years, despite the rumors that filtered through town while I was away, and unfortunately, still do. I've been invited to join committees at the school, locals talk to me as if I never left, and I'm lucky enough that my three older brothers have all fallen in love over the last two years, so I now have what I feel like are sisters. Considering they are all engaged now, it's basically a done deal.

Something much, *much* needed in my life.

I didn't really have friends back in Boston. Which helped in a way. I didn't leave anyone behind, except Colter, Max's father, and his family.

And good riddance to his parents. They might be Max's grandparents and treat him like a prince, but to me they were nothing but toxic.

Then again, they never saw me as more than the seventeen-year-old girl whom their son knocked up while on vacation eight years ago.

Max and I moving back here was a choice Colt and I made together.

It was the best one.

We didn't belong on the East Coast, living the big city life.

I didn't belong.

"Hi, Sandy," I say and take a seat, sliding the tray of cupcakes onto the table filled with cookies, cakes, fruit cups, and snack trays.

Then I look out into the school's parking lot and smile.

It might be a silly thing to celebrate, but that's one of the reasons I love living in a small town.

That and the only things Max and I have to do each day are the things *we* decide to do.

"Oh, more cupcakes with frosting—the kids will love them," Sandy says, and I glance over the table once more.

There's only one other set of cupcakes. They're adorable, too, and look professionally frosted with just the perfect number of sprinkles on each one.

Heck, I sort of want to eat one of those over my own.

"Who else brought cupcakes?" I ask, admiring them.

"Declan. Only he added sprinkles to his to give them more color."

Ugh.

"He's such a good dad, making time to bake for his daughter," she adds and leans over to one of the other moms. "Did you hear that he's trying to buy out another tech company or something? That man is impressive."

"And doing it all on his own as a single dad. He's amazing."

And that right there is the reason my distaste with Declan resumed the moment I moved back.

The town's golden boy is even shinier now because he can do all these things as a single dad.

Here I am, a single mom with my own company as well, baking desserts for my kid, too, but that's okay. I'll just go fuck off because that's what's required of a single mom.

"How lovely." I force a smile. Then I turn to look out at the students to hide my true feelings.

I've been told my facial expressions speak louder than words. It's something I'm working on.

"Isn't he dreamy?" Cami Anderson leans in as she sits down. "It was his idea to do the water guns."

My gaze instantly falls to Declan playing with the kids. There are seven of them spraying him with water, drenching his shirt enough that it sticks to his chest, displaying every hard ridge of his sculpted body and drawing my attention to the full sleeve tattoo on his right arm.

I hate to admit that I like it. I like that it has flowers and trees and that every piece of art somehow comes back to his daughter.

I look to my right and then my left. Every mom around and even a couple of dads are staring at him.

I bite my lip to keep myself from saying something crude.

We are here for the kids, not to drool over one of the fathers. Even if he has a body that belongs on a magazine cover.

I have a grudge against the guy, but I'm not blind to how gorgeous he is.

One might even say sexy, but it won't be me.

Not out loud.

Suddenly, the laughter of my own child steals my attention. None other than Suzette Young is spraying him with water. We call her Susie, though. She's the total opposite of her father in every way. She's also my son's best friend.

She's the number one reason my son has loved every moment of moving away from his friends to a town he remembered only from family vacations.

You'd think I would have made amends with Declan by now because of our kids, but nope.

I'm an adult. A thriving one, too, but no part of me is ready to cross that bridge. Yet.

I know it's coming, though. I can't be petty forever.

"I just love that he made time to be here today," one of the moms says.

Or … can I?

"Mom!" Max runs up to me and I instantly squeal. He's soaking wet and I know he's about to come shake his shaggy dark brown hair on me. "Can Susie come over after school?"

Over his shoulder is a blonde girl his height with big blue eyes, grinning at me.

Susie.

My initial instinct is to say yes, but then a six-foot shadow falls over her as her father steps up behind her.

My eyes fall to his tattooed arms and travel upward, taking in his sculpted muscles, the way he stands with such confidence. His ocean-blue eyes shining under his backward hat are focused on me.

My gaze sweeps over his shirt and dark blue jeans and falls to his shoes before I finally return my attention to Max.

"I'm sure her dad has something fun planned for her, it being the last day of school and all. Another night, okay?"

Max lets out an exaggerated sigh but nods.

Guilt hits me immediately.

"Okay, parents!" Principal John says into a megaphone. "It's time for the traditional challenge against your kids. The tug-of-war!"

Kids start to cheer, and parents slowly rise from their seats.

What's happening?

This wasn't a thing when I was a kid.

"Come on, Mom," Max says with a big smile.

I love his smile, and I love even more that I have seen it every day since he made a friend.

I follow behind him, taking the other parents' lead.

"Alright, parents, line up opposite your kids. Max, you're at the front on the kids' side, so Ruby, that means you're at the front for the parents and so on," Principal John clarifies and then starts shouting orders toward another area of the parking lot.

Max gets in line, and more kids do the same. I stand waiting while my son makes silly faces at me. I return them, of course.

"Are we ready?" Principal John asks. I spot Susie behind Max and then freeze. If Susie is behind Max, then that means …

Slowly, I look over my shoulder.

Yep, there's Declan. Right behind me. His eyes are crossed, and his cheeks are puffed out. He is clearly making faces at my son now.

I poke him.

"Stop."

"Jesus, Ruby." Declan holds his hand to his side where I poked him. "Was that your nail?"

"Focus."

He holds his hands up in surrender. "It's just a fun kids' game. Lighten up."

I narrow my gaze at him and then spin around.

Max gives me a thumbs-up, and the principal starts a countdown from five.

I grip the rope and plant my feet.

"Go!"

I pull with all my might, as I assume the parents behind me do as well.

"Young! Pull for all of us!" someone from the back shouts.

"I'm trying!" he shouts back.

I tug harder, backing up when suddenly, two big arms wrap around me to grab the rope where my hands are.

"Hey, what are you doing?" I snap, feeling Declan's body press against my backside.

"I'm getting a better grip." His breath skirts across the skin of my neck.

Goosebumps pepper over my entire body.

"You can't just ... just ..."

"Do you want to win or not?' he says coolly into my ear.

"Of course. But you can't just take over like this."

"From the shouts behind us, it sounds like they are relying on me."

"Well, back up and let me help," I snap and then plant my feet and stick out my ass to make him back up.

He grunts, and suddenly, his right hand sweeps across my stomach to hold me in place.

"Careful, Ruby. If you keep backing up, I won't be able to focus."

"Real mature," I comment just as Max and Susie scream, "Now!"

All the kids holding the rope let go.

It happens in a flash. The feeling of being pulled backward, losing my footing and falling, only to land with my butt in Declan's lap.

His hands rest on either side of my hips.

"Shit," he groans.

"Oh my God." I roll off him. When I get to my knees, I find him lying flat on the ground.

I cringe. That had to hurt, but I quickly calm my expression, because this is still Declan and I don't feel bad for him. Ever.

"If you hadn't pulled so hard, this wouldn't have happened."

He lets out a breath and then rises to a seated position, bringing his face close to mine.

"You're welcome for the catch."

"The catch?"

"Yeah, your ass is in my lap, so you didn't hit the asphalt."

I roll my eyes and stand. "You—"

"We got you guys good!" Max cheers next to me, and then he and Susie give each other a high five.

"Want to come over later?" Susie asks, and the principal starts dismissing everyone as long as they have a parent.

Max's big doe eyes stare up at me.

I can't take it.

"Okay, but not all night."

"Yes!" both kids cheer and race to the treats table.

"You were going to tell him no again, weren't you?" Declan says next to me and bumps my shoulder as we watch our children fill a to-go plate with enough treats to keep them awake till midnight.

"No."

"I think you were."

"I wasn't."

"Hmm, I still disagree."

I side-eye him and walk off without a reply, but unfortunately, he follows.

"I'm thinking about grilling steaks for dinner tonight, if you and Max want to join us."

"Nope."

"I want a steak," Max says, joining us with his plate of treats.

"I've already got dinner in the Crock-Pot."

"Then you guys can eat with us!" Max cheers.

"No, no," I say before he can get too excited.

"Why not, Mom? We never eat with them except on Sundays, and they live right next door."

"That's not a reason to eat with them, Max. Mr. Willis lives on the other side of us, and you don't worry about eating with him."

"Yeah, because he's old and would just yell at me the whole time or tell me to keep my voice down."

He's not wrong. Mr. Willis is old, and time and time again, I have to tell him to turn his hearing aids down.

"Another time."

"You always say that."

I glance at Declan. He and Susie are still standing right near us, but he's pointing to something and not paying any attention to us.

"Max."

"Please, Mom."

His pleading voice hits me right in the heart. For him, I can't let my distaste for Declan get in the way of everything.

"Okay. We can all eat together."

Both kids cheer because, of course, Susie was listening.

They hurriedly walk in the direction of our houses.

I start to walk behind them, and Declan falls into line with me.

I let out an annoyed sigh at the same time he lets out a low whistle.

"That one hurt, didn't it?"

I ignore him.

He leans in to say, "Willingly agreeing to do something that includes hanging out with me pains you, doesn't it?"

"Do you have to talk right now?"

"I do. It's polite to chat when you're on a walk with someone."

"We are not on a walk. I am walking home, and you are following me."

"Because I live next door."

"Dang it," I say and snap my fingers.

Declan chuckles but quickens his steps to move in front of me.

"Seriously though, Ruby, why don't you like me? Tell me so that I can fix it."

I pause to look up at him, and those ocean-blue eyes stare back at me, begging me to put him out of his misery and spill the truth that he's asked me no less than fifty times over the last year.

Sometimes I wonder what it would be like to just forget that everyone compared my success to his during school or that people still think he is the greatest gift to this town and commend his ability to be a basic responsible adult that holds a job and feeds his kid, and just become friends with him to appease the children and my family, who all like Declan.

But then I think about how I left this town at seventeen to have my son and raise him with a life that includes both his mother and father. I sold my soul to Max's grandparents in exchange for graduating from high school on time, getting into a college that would help me start and run my own graphic design business, all so that I could one day be financially stable enough to bring us back here and give my son a life he could fall in love with. One *I* could fall in love with. I took lemons and made lemonade, but no one cares that I made a sacrifice to get where I am.

No, they just whisper to each other that I got pregnant by some rich kid and followed the money.

They don't know that I cried most nights, wishing my mom

were still here to tell me what to do or missing my dad and brothers, and the only way I could push past the loneliness of my situation was by loving my son and working my ass off to change the situation I put us in.

So no, I'm not going to tell him so that he can fix it.

I haven't needed anyone this far.

And I sure as hell don't need anyone now.

I just … I wish that someone, I don't know, saw me for me and not as the woman they think they know.

"Every time you ask me that, I'm going to add another year that I don't tell you," I finally answer him.

"Why? I'll be a hundred at this point or dead."

"Exactly," I say and walk around him to prepare for a dinner I'm only hosting to make my son happy.

DECLAN AND SUSIE have come to our house dozens of times for a meal, and yet, this one feels different. Unlike Sunday breakfast when my entire family is here, this meal includes only the four of us, and for a reason I can't explain, it makes me nervous.

I've just finished setting the table when the back door opens.

This is how Susie always comes over, but I half expected Declan to use the front door.

I knew I shouldn't have let my father put a gate between our yards.

According to the kids, it's like a secret passageway from house to house.

Anyway, Declan stepping through the back door makes me pause.

"Please, come on in like you own this house."

He chuckles, steps back out, and knocks on the frame.

"Hey, Ruby, can I come in?"

"No."

He chuckles louder and walks in.

"See, now, some days I just can't tell if you're being mean or flirting."

"Oh, it's the former, trust me."

He shrugs.

"If you say so. It sounds flirty, and I think I like it."

Before I can reply, Susie comes bouncing in after him, a tray of leftover cupcakes in her hand.

I eye them, then look away, hating how it excites me that she brought them.

Max takes them from her and sets them on the counter.

"Oh, wow. You have the whole setup. Plates out, food ready to serve, and everything."

"The sooner you sit, the sooner you leave," I point out in a hushed tone, since the kids are nearby and he clearly can't figure that part out on his own.

"What's for dinner?" Max asks.

"Mississippi mud roast."

"Did you make mashed potatoes?" he asks and turns to Susie, "You'll want the mashed potatoes instead of the diced ones."

"Okay." She grins and sits next to her dad.

"Yes, I made them," I say as I place them on the table with the other dishes so that we don't have to treat this like a buffet.

"Yes!" Max cheers once I set the fresh-from-the-oven garlic bread in front of him. "I was hoping this would show up soon." He turns his attention to Declan. "My mom is the best baker in town."

"I thought your mom's friend Brooke was the best?"

I shoot a glare at the man, who chose to sit at the head of the table, and looks ready to dig in.

Although now that I think of it, this is Declan. I shouldn't have put in any extra energy to serve him food.

Alas, the kids are present, and I'm still a mother who, 90 percent of the time, needs to show how mature she is.

"Go wash your hands," Declan says in his dad voice, nodding to the sink for Susie.

"You, too, Max."

The kids leave, and he smiles. I roll my eyes extra hard.

"One day," he repeats, and I pretend that I can't hear him.

"All set?" I ask after the kids come back.

I serve Max and Susie, then I serve myself before I sit back down.

"Mom, you forgot Declan."

I definitely did not.

"Whoops," I say, and Declan holds his plate out with a smile.

I look him in the eye.

You're annoying.

He stares back.

You like it.

I fill his plate half full and set it down in front of him.

"I'm going to need more than that."

Just when I think he's about to say something else, Susie cuts in. "Dad, manners."

I press my lips together to keep from laughing, but yeah, Declan, manners.

"You're absolutely right, Susie. Thank you, Ruby. This smells amazing. It's been a while since we had a meal like this."

"What? Cooked?"

Max laughs, and I wink at him.

At least my kid thinks I'm funny.

"One where we sit down and all the food is on the table."

"Didn't you go to Wind Valley and see your parents over the

holidays?" I immediately regret that I know a small detail like this about him.

It's hard not to know these little things when he's become such good friends with my brothers.

"Yeah, but my family, whom I love to death, didn't grow up with this style of meals. We made a plate and sat at the counter, or made a plate and watched TV."

"Every night?"

"Most. Both of my parents worked full days while I grew up, so they were tired by the time they came home and cooked dinner. Plus, my dad had to drive to and from Wind Valley each day for his job, so he was always walking in just as my mom and I finished eating."

"Oh, I didn't know that. Is that why you stuck to yourself during school?"

He pauses mid-bite.

"These sure are a lot of questions for dinner."

"Do you not like questions?"

Because if he doesn't, I have a whole list for him.

I smile. "I'm just making conversation."

He nods slowly.

We both glance at the kids, who seem to be in their own world as they eat.

"Yeah, it was. They worked hard, and my playing any kind of sport would have been one more thing they needed to plan their days around, so I chose computers. I didn't have to go anywhere but my room for that."

"Hmm."

"What?"

"Nothing."

"Come on, tell me what you're thinking."

"I'm not thinking about anything."

He erupts into laughter.

"That's unlikely."

I open my mouth to say more, but Max beats me to it.

"Mom, can we play a game after we get done eating?"

"Oh, maybe another night."

"So they can come have dinner with us again?"

"One game tonight is fine."

"Yes!" Both kids shovel the rest of their food into their mouths and then grab the simplest game in the game cabinet in the living room.

Guess Who.

The kids play a couple of warm-up rounds, as they call it, while Declan and I finish eating.

"Do you want help with the dishes?" Declan asks. I shake my head.

"I'll do them after you leave."

"Don't be silly. I'll help."

"No, thanks."

"Do we have to keep score?" Susie shouts from the living room.

"Nope. There is only first and second place on this one. It should be easy to track," Declan answers her as he makes his way to the coffee table. He and Susie sit on one side of the couch, while Max and I sit on the floor.

First and second place. I can tell you this, in my house, I better be the one coming in the first-place spot.

"Rock, paper, scissors to see who goes first," Max says.

I settle in, waiting for him and Susie to battle, but neither moves.

"Dad, that's you and Ruby."

"Oh, we have to do it?" he asks, clearly on the same thought train as me.

"Yes." Susie glances between us.

Declan scoots to the edge of the couch, flips his hat backward, and then rests his forearms on his thighs.

Palms flat, fists closed, Declan and I chant, "Rock, paper, scissors … shoot."

Both rocks.

"Rock, paper, scissors … shoot."

Both papers.

The kids laugh.

"Rock, paper, scissors … shoot."

"Yes!" I squeal. My rock covers his scissors.

Declan chuckles, and Max gives me a high five.

It's so dumb and no one knows it but me, but I beat Declan at something and I am elated.

"Way to start strong, Mom."

We set up, draw our characters, and Max rubs his hands together and laughs when he sees who we have.

I have no idea where he gets his competitiveness from.

Max and Susie battle back and forth, knocking down people with glasses or hats or white hair, leaving us with just a few possible candidates.

"Okay, the last question is for the parents," Max says, and Susie giggles.

"Dad, you're up."

After what feels like ages, Declan asks, "Does your person have a mustache?"

That answer is going to reveal our person. I won't even get a chance to ask a question myself.

I glance at the card, then at the kids, then at Declan.

A smug smile appears on his lips. "You're Max, aren't you?"

I don't reply, and he grabs my card.

"I knew it." He chuckles, and Susie leaps onto him to give him a hug. "How does second place feel?"

Talk about triggers.

I open my mouth, praying that the 90 percent comes out, but Susie is faster.

"Dad, no. We do not talk like that. Poor sportsmanship is not welcome in our house."

I'm suddenly filled with pure joy at watching his daughter scold him.

"I … this isn't our house," he argues, then has the audacity to look at me and wink.

"Same rules apply," I grin and cross my arms.

"Yeah," Max adds.

"Yeah," Susie also adds.

We all quickly agree that, from here on out, we will not tease each other for losing. We play two more games, and Max and I lose those, too.

Soon after, Declan and Susie go home, and Max and I prepare for bed.

Once he's fast asleep, I slip into my pajamas, wash my face, and grab my laptop before crawling into bed to work for a couple more hours.

Business has been good for me, which is saying a lot now that AI can do almost anything I can.

But that also means I need to work harder now more than ever to ensure I continue to find new clients and don't lose my current ones.

I can't afford to.

Not when the final piece to having full control over my life again is paying off the money I accepted from Colter's family to send me to college. I'd wanted to believe they were good people so badly that I agreed to a personal loan from Colter's dad instead of using an actual bank.

God, I was so naive to trust them.

But guess what?

Lesson learned.
Trust from Ruby Asher doesn't come easy.
Not anymore.
I'll never be that girl again.

CHAPTER TWO

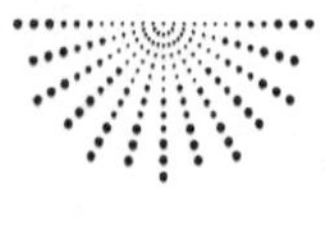

DECLAN

"You have the final numbers?" I ask, looking at my computer screen and into the face of Steven, my executive assistant at the antivirus company I created that eventually exploded into more ventures in the industry.

"Yes, an email with our offer is being drafted as we speak."

"Good. I need this to happen discreetly and quickly."

"Yes, sir."

"Call me as soon as you hear back or if there are any hiccups."

"Yes, sir."

"And Steven, there better not be any."

"No, sir."

I end the Zoom and then rub a hand over my face.

Sir.

I fucking hate when they call me that, but I like that they respect me enough to use it.

I close my browser and switch to my email as soon as the notice comes through. I review it quickly, pleased with how things are turning out.

My company is in the top three for my line of work. There's Collins Corporation, Davenport Inc., and my company, Young Technologies,

Now, all of us have investments in different areas of the tech world, but if you've heard of it, one of these three companies more than likely owns it.

In the past fiscal year, the competition between my company and Davenport Inc. has increased substantially, and the only solution that I believe will put me at the top is buying out Collins Corp.

The first offer, of many I'm sure, since much more goes into this, has just been sent.

If I can secure this before Devonport gets wind of it, it'll be pure luck.

And that's what I'm aiming for right now.

Fuck, if I can just make this happen, the past few years will all have been worth it.

And I *need* it to be worth it.

Suddenly, the patio door slides open with a bang.

"Quick! Hide this!" My daughter's voice squeaks with excitement as she runs through the back door and into the kitchen.

I glance up from my makeshift office at the kitchen table just in time to see Max, her best friend, come sprinting behind her, a smile on his face. His run is a mixture of skips and actually running, and the glint in his eyes says they are up to something they shouldn't be.

"Cabinet, cabinet, cabinet." He follows her.

I rise and pull off my glasses, catching the exact moment Susie clumsily attempts to put what appears to be a Tupperware of something into said cabinet.

I let out a sigh.

"Did Ruby bake something again?"

Two sets of innocent eyes, one bright green and the other ocean blue, turn to me.

"Blueberry lemon cookies," Susie whispers as her lips stretch into a smile.

I blow out my breath.

Damn. Those sound delicious.

I move toward the kids, ready to ask them my routine list of questions, because this is not the first time something like this has happened. In fact, for the last few months, it's been a weekly event on Saturday mornings. I was sure they would tire of it and it would stop, but I clearly was mistaken.

My lips part, ready to do my thing, when Susie cracks open the lid and holds the container to my face.

I'm distracted by the sweet smell of sugar and blueberries. I take a deep breath.

"You know you want to try it," Max says. The last word ends with a little higher pitch than the rest.

I do. He's not wrong, but that's not the point here. The point is, these two steal Ruby's desserts on the weekly and hide them here, which then starts a fight, if we want to call it that, between her and me.

It's more like she's annoyed, and I enjoy watching her get worked up, so I play into it.

The woman is determined to hate me no matter what I choose to do, so I may as well get some joy out of it.

To be fair to the kids, it's really not that hard to upset Ruby when it comes to anything related to me. Susie could be caught tie-dyeing on Ruby's white table, staining the wood surface a shit brown, and Ruby would tell her it's okay, that accidents happen and she can fix it, but the moment I step into the house, she'd tell me I can properly wait outside.

All because once upon a time, I pissed her off and she never let it go.

Her brothers ask me on the regular what I did to their little sister and I tell them *if only I knew myself*.

Why Ruby Asher can't stand me remains a mystery.

You'd think that because of that, I wouldn't be attracted to her.

But unfortunately for me, I am.

I'm attracted to a lot of things about her.

It's fucking annoying.

"Come on, Dec. Try it," Max insists.

I hold my hands up and step back, as if that's going to help.

"No, no. Did you two ask before you took these?"

Susie rolls her eyes and crosses her arms.

"Yes, Dad, we asked if we could have them. We asked how many we could have. We asked if we could borrow the container, and we asked if … I could share with you." Susie smirks. "Her answer took a little longer on that one, but she did say that I could."

"Did she?" I raise one brow at them as Max hands me a cookie.

"She sure did." Max grins.

I cave, and take a bite, closing my eyes and letting the warm cookie melt in my mouth. My taste buds burst with every flavor.

Ruby is a gifted baker, but I will never tell her so. You know, because I have to play the part of hated neighbor and all that.

"Max!"

Just as I'm taking bite number two, my mouth still open, Ruby's voice rings through the backyard and into my kitchen. She appears at the still-open sliding patio door.

She pauses, her bright green eyes taking in the scene. One kid, mine, sitting on the counter in her pink jean shorts and yellow shirt, hair in a messy ponytail, a Tupperware bowl in her lap and me standing in front of her wearing nothing but a pair of gray sweats and a black baseball hat, barefoot, eating a cookie and staring at her with wide eyes as if I was caught doing something wrong.

Which, I'm expecting, will be the case. As usual.

Her gaze darts over the room but stalls on my bare chest.

I take pride in making sure I eat right and stay active daily, but with the way her eyes linger on me, I'm sure she's thinking I somehow screwed that up, too.

Then the little boy next to me takes off down the hall. Susie and I both turn our heads to watch him go.

"Maxwell Miles Davenport, get your booty back out here," Ruby scolds. Then she clears her throat.

As if we are mirrors, Susie and I look back at Ruby.

She smooths her hands over her baking apron and holds her head high in my doorframe.

"Well, are you going to invite me in?"

I know I shouldn't, but I bark out a laugh.

"Your kid practically lives here. I don't think inviting you into my house is necessary anymore. You can just walk in, Ruby."

Her gaze narrows, and she steps in.

"I don't appreciate you implying that my kid is here with you more than he's with me."

I finally take the bite I'd been going for, chew a couple of times, and say, "That, by no means, was what I said."

And it's not. One of the many things that attracts me to Ruby is her approach to mothering.

She's a fucking great one.

Phenomenal, really. How she does all that and stays sane is beyond me.

I hope people tell her that. Lord knows, this town makes sure to tell me anytime I step out of the house.

You're such a good dad, Declan. Susie is so lucky.

It pisses me off.

Yeah, if she's so lucky, why didn't her mom stick around? Oh, that's right, she left because of me.

I'm the problem. I'm the reason Susie doesn't have a mom, and it fucking kills me every day. Every compliment only makes the wound deeper.

"Well, it sounded like—" Her gaze flicks to my daughter, and everything in Ruby's face shifts from deep wrinkles of frustration to even calmness. If that's even a thing for her.

Susie is also eating a cookie.

"Do you think the lemon was too much?" Ruby asks, and Susie shakes her head.

"These are so good. They might be my new favorite."

"Wonderful."

"I won't lie. I think—"

"I was talking to Susie," Ruby says in the sweetest voice, shooting a wink at her, then following her son down the hall.

Susie nudges my leg with her foot.

"I think she likes you," my daughter whispers, and like before, my laugh is loud and deep.

Yeah, no. That's not it. Not even close.

"Why are you laughing, Dad? Don't kids tease the ones they like? You told me that once."

Shit. I did.

I grab the container, snap the lid back on it. "I think her son did something wrong and she's upset. Care to share what that was and if you were a part of it?"

Susie shakes her head.

"I see. That's how it's going to be, huh?"

No response.

I put the cookies in the cupboard and lift my daughter off the counter and over my shoulder, one hand holding her in place and the other tickling her side.

"To the trampoline we go!" I say, and Susie instantly squirms with laughter.

"No, no, last time you bounced me, I thought I was going to go over the net."

Facts. I might have gone a little too hard that day, but she was having fun, and her giggles were so infectious.

Nothing motivates me more than my daughter's happiness.

It will always be my priority. No matter what people say.

"Looks like this will be attempt number two." I let out an exaggerated evil laugh.

"No, no! Okay, I'll tell you."

I slow my steps on the back patio. We stand in front of each other. I cross my arms, and she mimics me.

"Max spilled the salt cup into the second batch of cookies and didn't tell his mom. So, we took cookies from batch one and rushed them over here to be sure we got the good ones before she found out."

I don't really have any follow-up questions aside from who has a cup of salt sitting around and not a shaker, but that's not exactly what needs to be addressed right now.

"Did you see him do it?"

Susie's bright smile fades.

She nods.

"And you didn't tell Ruby?"

She shakes her head.

"Should you have told Ruby?"

She nods.

"I agree. Now, let's go get the rest of the cookies we have and give them back to her."

"Alright."

With her head hanging low, Susie heads back into the house.

I take a moment for myself.

Susie is a good kid. The best, in fact. Even Max is one of a kind, considering that his mother is one of the most uptight people I know.

But they are still kids, and they make mistakes and need a lesson, no matter how small.

Being a single dad is challenging, and I just loathe making my daughter sad.

Some days, I wish Susie's mother had stuck around for Susie's sake.

In the end, her mother told me I work too much and she was tired of taking the backseat to a dream I was never going to achieve. It didn't hurt when she said she wanted to leave me, but it killed me when she told me to go ahead and keep Susie.

To keep her.

As if she were the fucking suede couch we bought together and only one of us could take it with us.

She had no intention of being a part of Susie's life when she left, and she left because of me.

Susie cried every night for weeks.

Those nights are forever engraved in my memory and somewhere along the way, I vowed to finish what I started. Achieve my goals. The ones that drove her mom away.

I wasn't about to let all that hard work be for nothing.

To let that loss in my daughter's life be for nothing.

Once my mind was made up, moving back to Lovers only made sense. I'd reach my goal and slow down enough to make more time for my kid.

Yes, finding a balance has been difficult, but I refuse to give up.

Especially since my daughter's smile has been constant since the day we moved into this house, and it's only grown by having her best friend next door.

Sure, things will be different once Ruby's brother and my

friend Luca, who is building a house for us, is finished and we live across town, but this town is where we are meant to be.

I head toward the laughter coming from inside my kitchen and pause in the doorway. Ruby is holding the cookies while both kids chase her.

All three of them are grinning, eyes shining with joy. Ruby has discarded her apron onto the counter, revealing her white lacy top and linen shorts.

Here's the thing about Ruby. She pushes my buttons daily with her snarky remarks. We don't get along despite the act we put up in front of the kids, and yet … everything about her screams my type.

Smart, witty, long lean legs, strawberry blonde hair that shines in the sun, emerald eyes that captivate you, and a smile that almost makes me forget how much she annoys me. Like me, she's started her own business, and from what her brothers and a quick Google search have told me, she's quite successful with it, too. It's a little embarrassing how sexy I find all these things about her. About a woman who can't stand me.

Ruby pauses, letting the kids catch her and tackle her to the living room rug.

It's as cheesy a scene as it gets, but one thing is certain.

I'll put up with the scolding, the snapbacks, the arguing, and the way Ruby's smile complicates every emotion I have for her on a daily basis if it gives Susie more moments like this.

"Dad!" Susie hollers when she sees me. "Ruby said we can keep the cookies."

Everyone settles down, and Ruby and Max head for the door.

I step back to let them through, but Ruby stops right in front of me.

"There was one rule, of course." She looks at Susie with a grin.

"I can keep them as long as I am the only one who eats them." My daughter lets out a laugh. "I said, no problem!"

I glance at Ruby with an *are you serious?* look, and she shrugs before she walks out the door.

I close the door behind them, and Susie climbs back onto the counter, peeking out the window over the sink.

We both watch as Ruby and Max disappear through the fence.

Once they are gone, Susie grins and tosses me the container.

"Don't tell Ruby," she says.

"Deal."

Container in hand, we head for the living room to settle in with snacks and a movie.

We're about fifteen minutes into K-Pop Demon Hunters for the hundredth time when my phone pings with an email notification.

I jump up immediately and move for my computer, which is still where I left it in the kitchen.

I open the email, read quickly, and ball my fists with each word.

Turns out, I'm not the only one trying to purchase the Collins Corporation.

CHAPTER THREE

RUBY

One of my favorite things about moving back to Lovers has been watching the relationship between Max and my brothers grow.

With Luca, he's learning how to build and repair things. With Hudson, he's learned how to skate on ice and pretty much any other kind of hockey move Hudson is willing to teach. With Miles, the brother who was always the first to play with me as a kid, Max has learned how to change a tire, change the oil in multiple car models, and to slow down in the day to day. That last one still blows my mind. Miles used to be all about structure, but since he fell in love with Quinn, he's all about experiences and not taking life too seriously.

To be honest, I think all of my brothers have shown him this in one way or another.

So, when all three of them showed up at my door at seven in the morning to steal Max away for a lake day, I couldn't say no. Not that I was planning to.

I have a to-do list a mile long.

As soon as they left, I started from the top of my checklist.

Food. Our house needs food.

I give myself twenty minutes to get in and out of the grocery store, but with the way Mrs. Whittaker is looking at me, I don't think it's going to happen.

"Hi there, Ruby." She waves at me and then blocks my shopping cart with her own. "I can't tell you enough how delightful it is to have you back in Lovers. We all missed you while you were gone."

She has told me this every time she's seen me in the last year.

Either she wants me to really know this, she forgot that she told me, or she's hoping that by bringing it up again, I'll reveal the true reason I left in the first place. You know, so she can be the first to spread the news.

Still, this is Mrs. Whittaker. A nosey old woman who is sweeter than a jar full of sugar. I've never been anything but kind, despite her motives for repeating herself to me.

"Thank you, Mrs. Whittaker. I appreciate hearing that."

"Don't leave us again, okay?"

I smile and nod, "If I have a say in it, I won't."

"Wonderful. Enjoy your afternoon."

She pushes her cart down the aisle and disappears around the corner.

Short and sweet. Just how I like it.

Lovers is a small town, so I know they all know why I left after Max was born, but they don't know the whole story, which is why most of them believe I left solely for financial reasons.

Yes, I had a choice back then, but it was different.

I was young and scared.

I also thought I was in love.

When Max was born, his father didn't live here. His family vacationed at Lovers Lodge multiple times a year, but it wasn't going to be enough for Colter. I went to Lovers High School; he went to a private school on the East Coast and was set to earn multiple scholarships. Colter (or his family) moving here didn't make sense. So they made me an offer. If I moved to Boston, I'd live with them, they'd pay for me to go to the same private school as Colter, they would hire a nanny to watch Max so we could both graduate as planned, they would pay for me to go to college, and we'd both get to be a part of Max's life every single day.

Of course, it all came at a price. That family doesn't just give you something and expect nothing in return.

Being a mom at seventeen is hard, but having someone ask you to leave everything you know in life is harder. But I tried to focus on how it would bring me to moments like the one I'm in now.

I have a degree and started my own graphic design company at twenty, and now I'm living back in my hometown the way I always dreamed I would.

I just wish I didn't have to stress about money like I have lately.

I'm lucky that my dad is letting me live in his house so that I can save on rent, but I'm still out that money I owe to the Davenports.

God, I cannot wait to have that paid off.

I have to find a way to make some extra income this summer.

My phone rings, bringing me out of the daydream of the past.

I pull it from my purse and grin.

"Hello, this is unusual timing for you."

The voice on the other end of the line chuckles.

"I had a break in my day and thought I'd call. Is Max around? Can I talk to him?"

I pause my cart to grab some cans off the shelf before I answer Colt's questions.

His family would have a hernia if they heard Max and I call him anything other than Colter.

"Luca picked him up early this morning to go to the lake. They took Susie with them."

"Whoa, Luca is taking one for the team and watching two kids?"

"No. Miles and Hudson are there and probably Declan, too." He chuckles again.

"You really don't like this guy, do you? I feel the pain when you have to say his name all the way through the phone."

"I have my reservations about him, yes. But his kid is cute and extra sweet."

"I like that Max has a best friend."

"Me too."

"Alright, well, when you see him, have him call me. I want to ask him about the last blast. I saw pictures on the website, and I want to ask him about the tug-of-war."

I halt.

"What pictures?"

"Well, to start, there is one of all the parents lying on the ground with the kids laughing. You're full on sitting on some guy's lap, but honestly, by his size compared to yours, he probably didn't notice."

"Oh, he noticed and so did I. It was horrible."

"Whoa, hold on, is that Declan?"

"Mmm."

"I finally have a face to the name. This is great. Let me pull it up again real fast."

"Why?"

"So I can confirm … yeah, you're right. His face is super annoying."

I snort. The woman next to me stares for a moment but then keeps walking with a small wave.

I wave back.

"What's this guy's last name again?"

"Young. Why?"

"It just sounds familiar."

"Probably because Max talks about Susie so much. I'm sure her dad's name comes up."

He hums on the other end. "Yeah, I guess. So, hey, listen, my dad mentioned that he emailed you last week about work—did you get it?"

"Mm-hmm."

"And you didn't reply?"

"No. I did not. He wanted to know how my numbers were this last quarter, and I don't think it's any of his business."

"I'm sure he's only asking because …"

"Because he wants to make sure I don't miss a payment to him. I know."

I missed a payment over the holidays, and they will never, ever forget it.

Like I said, I need to find a way to make extra money this summer. The sooner I pay his parents back, the sooner I'll never have a reason to see or talk to them again unless it's for Max.

"I know how he can be. I'm sorry, Ruby."

How my son's father came from such a pill of a man is beyond me.

"It's not your fault. I'm the one who agreed to this."

"Yeah, I sort of thought they'd let it go once you graduated, though. Lord knows, my family can afford it."

I thought so, too, but the moment Colt and I announced that we weren't going to continue dating, it was like a switch flipped. I was now the enemy, and they weren't going to let me go without making sure I knew it.

"I wish you'd just let me pay it off for you."

"No," I say quickly, sorting through the containers of strawberries for a good batch. "If I pay them off, they will know I got the money somewhere else and start asking questions."

"Well, at that point, you'll have paid them off and it won't matter."

Valid, but not the point.

"I need to do it myself, okay? Letting you pay it off would just prove them right after all these years."

"Ruby," he says in a soft tone. "They don't—"

"They do," I cut him off.

The first night I was in Boston, I'd heard Colt fighting over me with his parents. They told him that I'd trapped him for his money. I was the youngest gold digger they'd ever met.

It seems I had that reputation going for me no matter where I was.

Lucky me.

"I'll have Max call you tonight," I change the subject quickly.

"Yeah, okay. I'll talk to you later, Ruby."

"Bye."

I hang up and drop my phone back into my purse.

When I turn the corner, my cart bumps into another. I freeze.

"Oh, I'm so sorry, I didn't … Declan. I thought you went to the lake with my brothers."

My gaze immediately falls to where his T-shirt hugs his biceps. But I catch myself before I check him out too much, and pull my cart back.

"Hudson offered a few hours free of Susie to get some things done, and I took it."

I cross my arms. "Same here."

"And yet we both end up doing the most riveting thing. Grocery shopping. We may as well have just driven together."

I scoff and head in the opposite direction.

"Come on, Ruby, admit you secretly like me."

His voice has a deeper tone right now. It always does when the kids aren't around.

Probably best, since the way he says my name in this tone makes my nipples harden and I'm not proud of it.

Not one bit.

"I do not."

"As a friend, at least."

I pause and turn to him. "You are friends with my brothers—that's it. I just deal with it like a mature adult would."

His head volleys.

"Well, I wouldn't say—"

"Do not finish that sentence."

He chuckles, which in turn leads me to roll my eyes.

Are my choices the most mature? Not exactly. But being near him brings out this side of me, and it's uncontrollable. And I'm a little on edge from my conversation with Colt.

"Hey, so the kids want another dinner game night rematch," Declan changes the subject.

"Oh, you two have dinner game nights?" Mrs. Whittaker pops up out of nowhere.

"No, no," I say quickly at the same time Declan says, "Not that way, no."

"Oooh." She shrugs with a grin I have seen more times than I'd like to admit on her face. "It just sounds like you two are playing house."

"Playing house?" I repeat, mortified.

"How did dinner and a game night become playing house?" Declan crosses his arms and pins the old lady with a look.

It's actually quite comical how serious he looks right now, but still, I'd like to know the answer as well.

"Oh, well, I ..."

"Mm-hmm, this is how rumors get started, Mrs. Whittaker." Declan shakes his finger at her, and she bows her head, looking a little embarrassed. "Ruby and I don't need anyone thinking we are more than we are."

"Which is …" the old lady asks, and I laugh.

She doesn't even try to hide how nosey she is.

"Nothing," I answer.

"Friends," Declan says at the same time.

I snap a glare at him.

"Okay. If you say so." Mrs. Whittaker pats his shoulder and keeps walking.

What happened to her cart?

"Please don't tell people we are friends," I groan.

"Why not? Would it be so bad?"

"Yes."

"Why?"

"Why do you care, Declan?"

Now it's his turn to shrug as he pretends to be fascinated with the marshmallows on the shelf in front of him.

"I … um, I think you *could* be cool," he finally says.

"*Could* be?"

He turns to me now with a grin.

"Yes. *Could* be. I mean, you do think I'm funny."

"Do I?"

He points at my face. "Well, you are smiling."

I drop the smile and groan.

"You're so annoying." I walk off, but Allie Simmons, the mom to one of the kids who'd been in Max and Susie's class, stops him.

"Declan, hi!" she says in a tone I can only describe as flirty. "Fancy running into you here."

It's a small town, Allie. We have one grocery store.

"Ah, yeah, well, kids got to eat and all that. Thought I'd make Susie her favorite for dinner tonight," he says. I look over my shoulder; he's watching me.

Our eyes lock just as Allie says, "Gosh, look at you just mastering this single dad life. What can't you do?"

I glance away and turn into the next row.

He's freaking grocery shopping and still winning medals.

Gah.

I finish my list, and by the time I check out, I have an answer for Allie.

You know what Declan Young can't do?

Convince me to be his friend.

CHAPTER FOUR

DECLAN

Summer at the lake in Wyoming was something I always missed while I was living in Chicago. Yeah, there were piers, but this is different. Lovers Lake feels more intimate and relaxing—less to worry about and more time to enjoy being in the moment.

Which is why when Luca asked if Susie and I wanted to have another lake day later that week, saying yes was a no-brainer.

However, I wasn't exactly aware that Ruby would be here too. At the same time, it shouldn't surprise me. Now that all the Asher kids are living in the same town again, they make it a point to spend more time together.

My watch vibrates at the same time my phone dings. I glance at my wrist to read a text from Steven. He's been working with our PR team on the news that leaked of both my company and Davenport Inc. looking to purchase Collins Corporation. Too many media outlets want a comment on the feud it sparked. Little do they know that, for the past few years, all three compa-nies have been walking around to see who was going to light the match first.

Looks like we all got tired of waiting.

Susie hollers at me while I scan his text. It's just another update, same as the others over who has been reaching out.

"Dad, you said you wouldn't work today while we were at the beach." Her lips are turned down.

I did say that.

"I'm not," I reply and hold my hands up.

I can reply later. There is a reason Steven holds the position he does. He can handle this.

"Yay, okay, will you be on my volleyball team?" Susie runs up, kicking sand along the way.

She's clearly up to something.

Three.

Two.

One.

"My mom is going to be on my team," Max says, appearing at my daughter's side as if they were magnetized together.

I glance at the beach volleyball net, where Ruby and Miles lower the height for the kids. Ruby is wearing a black bikini today and it's—fuck, my thoughts right now should be illegal.

They're nothing compared to the ones I had when I saw her in the store a couple of days ago. There is just something about the long skirts she wears with shirts that stop just at her belly button, giving me a tease of the smooth skin of her stomach, that turns me on.

Then, I made her smile. A genuine smile.

But of course, one of the school moms walked up and ruined it.

Praising me for buying fucking food.

Blows my mind. Has this town never seen a single dad care for his child?

"You and me against them?" I ask, pushing those thoughts to the back of my mind.

"You, me, and Luca against Ruby, Max, and Miles."

"What about Shay and Quinn?" I ask. "Don't they want to play?"

"They are reading over there." Max points and sure enough, both ladies are lounging with books in their hands.

"Alright, let's do this."

"Careful now, Ruby has played this a time or two," Mr. Asher warns me, joining the party with a bucket filled with ice, beers, and bottles of water.

"Noted."

She's probably the only Asher sibling besides Hudson who has any kind of athletic skill.

But I'll never let the boys know that I think about that.

Boys basketball is sacred … you know, when we get around to playing it.

I follow Susie and Max to the net. An upbeat song is playing from Miles's Bluetooth speaker.

Luca is waiting at the side of the net. He points me toward the middle.

Ruby is directly across from me with a smirk.

"I've seen you play sports before," she teases in an attempt to get under my skin.

I let out a sarcastic laugh.

"But you've never seen me play volleyball."

"No, but I imagine with your age, it won't be easy."

"My age?" I nearly gasp. "I'm not that much older than you."

"Yes, you are."

"Eight years."

"Almost nine," she rebuttals.

"That's not much of an age gap," I defend myself.

"Oh, it is."

"No, it's not."

She shrugs. "I guess we can agree to disagree on whether that's a gap or not."

The nerve she has.

To make a show of how ready I am, I strip my shirt off and stretch one arm across my chest, followed by the other, my gaze never leaving Ruby's. I tilt my head side to side, hearing the crack but ignoring it. Next, I jump up and down, then side to side with a grin.

Warming up is necessary and—oh, fuck!

I rub the back of my head and spin. "Luca, did you just hit me in the head with the ball?"

"How was I supposed to know you were going to start jumping up and down during my serve?"

"Maybe look first."

"My bad." He laughs.

But it's not his laugh that consumes me—it's the one on the other side of the net.

"Solid start." Ruby grins.

"Solid start," I mimic her. Then I say in my normal voice, "Just be ready."

"If you say so."

I do say so, and now I'm determined to win.

Luca serves the ball again, this time making it over the net.

Miles bumps it low, Max hits it awkwardly, Ruby dives to save it and launches it over the net.

Luca is ready, bumping it to me. I bump it to Susie, who misses completely.

I instantly look at Ruby to make sure she isn't laughing.

She's not. She's squatting low so that Max can whisper in her ear.

"It's okay, Susie, you'll get them on the next one."

"I know." She nods quickly. She closes her eyes and mouths, "I can do this. I can do this."

"Ready?" Miles asks, already in position to serve.

"Ready!" Susie shouts.

This time, Luca bumps it, and I spike it over the net to Ruby, who blocks it instantly.

The ball falls back onto my side, at my feet.

She smiles.

Damn it, that was good.

"It's okay, Dad. You'll get the next one."

"Thank you, Susie."

"Okay, let's get serious," Luca says.

"I was serious," Ruby argues with her brother.

"I'm not playing if you two are going to argue," Miles adds and walks off.

"Anyone want ice cream?" Mr. Asher asks and both kids go running in his direction.

"I'm out, too, then." Luca moves to sit by Shay.

Ruby is still standing by the net.

"I guess that means we won." She shrugs. "Sorry, old man."

Old man.

I'm *not* old.

Looks like I'll just have to prove it.

"No way. One on one." I say, the words falling off my lips before I can think twice. "That didn't count."

"It counted. I won. You didn't."

"Rematch. One game. We each get to serve."

If I had to guess, her eyes are narrowing behind her sunglasses as she stares at me.

"Fine. One game."

"Ladies first." I pick up the ball and hand it to her under the net. She grabs it from me.

This will be fun.

I back up, making sure I can easily access all the space on my side.

Ruby, too, gets into position and looks at me.

I nod.

She nods.

Then she spikes it over the net.

I start gently with a bump.

After a couple of volleys, I spike it.

Ruby hits the sand, saving it and returning it to my side.

I spike it again, assuming she can't stand up fast enough, but I'm wrong.

She's quick to her feet and blocks it.

I'm quick, too, and I don't let this one hit the sand.

I send it back to her, she spikes, and I earn a face full of sand as the ball lands right next to me.

Ruby's cheers are followed by those from the rest of the group.

I didn't realize we had an audience.

"Now, this is the kind of game I wanted. Please resume." Miles waves a hand in the air.

I stand up quickly, ready for redemption.

Ball in hand, I serve it over.

Like before, Ruby bumps.

I bump.

Then Ruby spikes the ball with fury, and it hits me dead center in the face. I feel the blood rush down, over my lips and chin.

"Shit!" someone yells as I drop to my knees and cover my nose.

"Are you okay?"

"Damn, Ruby, how hard did you hit the ball?"

"Let me see it."

Quinn, Shay, and Miles all hover over me. They ask question after question, and I answer as best I can in rapid-fire response.

But my next words freeze on my tongue as Ruby drops to her knees next to me and places a wet towel to my face.

I reach up, my hand grazing hers, and our eyes lock as everyone fusses around us.

Normally, I can read the expression on her face, but right now, I can't.

"Are you okay?" she asks quietly. Again, her voice is void of any emotion, but her hands are shaking.

Oddly, I'm a little more concerned about her now.

She's always been easy for me to read.

I don't like this.

"I'm good."

"Good."

Although her answer is short, she doesn't pull her gaze from mine.

The others make their way back to their seats, and I lean closer to Ruby.

"Are you good?"

She nods.

"Are you sure?"

Another nod.

I use the napkin Ruby brought me to dab at my face. The bleeding has stopped.

"That was fun though," I tell Ruby. "Your dad said you've played before. Was it in high school?"

"Yep. Before I got pregnant, of course. I didn't realize how much I missed it."

A smile touches her lips.

"Wait, wait, wait. Does this … did you just have fun … with me?"

"No."

"I think you did."

"I enjoyed the challenge. Not you."

"Oh, I get it. You like to be challenged. I can work with that."

"Don't make this a thing."

"I'm not making it a thing."

"You are."

"I'm just saying that if you open yourself up to the idea of friends, things like this could happen more often."

"Me hitting you in the face with a ball?"

I bump her shoulder with mine.

"You having fun."

"I have fun."

"Do you?"

"I … let's just move on."

"Right. I told Max he was welcome to come over for movie night tonight if it was okay with you."

"Of course."

"You are welcome as well."

She laughs. "No, thank you."

Then she rushes off to help Shay and Quinn start packing up. My eyes shamelessly veer to her ass in her bikini. I give myself a good one, two count and look away.

I take a deep breath.

There's no point in being attracted to Ruby. She wants nothing to do with me.

And yet … I don't know why I'm determined to make Ruby my friend, but I am.

Maybe I like the challenge, too.

———

NOTHING BEATS a long cold shower after a day in the sun. I saunter down the steps to the living room. Susie is already curled up with a blanket and a large bowl of popcorn in front of her. Next to her are three bowls.

She grins innocently.

"Movies always have to come with popcorn, Dad."

I sigh. Some nights, there isn't any point in arguing with my daughter.

I flop into the recliner, lean forward to scoop up a bowl of buttery popcorn, and Max walks through the front door.

Ruby is right behind him.

"Are you sure you don't want to stay?" I ask. "It's Mario."

"I'm sure," Ruby says while Max makes a beeline for the couch to sit by Susie. They place the big bowl between them and both start eating as if we didn't feed them all day.

"Are you sure this is okay?" Ruby asks, crossing her arms in the doorway. "You're not tired or sore or anything and want to call it a day?"

I nod while the kids start to argue over who gets the remote.

"It's fine. I'm fine. If he starts to doze off, I'll send him home."

Ruby nods and then turns on her heel. I follow her out the front door.

"Or I can text you when he's ready, and you can come get him."

She nods, turning to face me as she takes the first step off my front porch. Her gaze trails from my gray sweatpants up to my face, stalling slightly on my bare chest the way it always does. Maybe that's why I keep not wearing one.

"Have I mentioned how much I hate that you have my phone number?"

I'm opening my mouth to respond when a blue car pulls up. It's still daylight, so it's not late by any means, but I wasn't expecting company.

The driver parks quickly and jogs toward us.

What is Logan, my landlord, doing here?

"Hi, Ruby. Hey, Declan. How's it going?"

"Fine."

"That's good. How's the packing going?" he asks.

I glance between Ruby and Logan. Who's packing what?

Ruby's brows dip toward her tiny nose.

"Are you asking me?" I ask.

Logan nods. "You got my email, didn't you?"

I step farther onto the porch and rest my hands on my hips as I stare at him.

"What email?"

Logan cringes. "The one with my thirty-day notice to vacate."

"Vacate," I snap. "This house?"

Logan nods. "The wife and I finally listed it."

"I'll pay you double in rent for the next three months to wait," I say instantly. I hate tossing money out this way, but this situation calls for it.

Luca swore my house would be ready by the end of the summer. I need him to be right.

Ruby grunts, but I ignore her.

"That would be amazing, Declan, but we accepted an offer this morning. It was word of mouth and sold quickly."

This can't be happening.

"Wait, so what are you saying? I now have less than a month to move?"

He nods, zero hints of guilt on his face.

"Two weeks, to be specific."

"Two weeks?"

Ruby rushes past me to close the front door so the kids don't hear me shouting.

I nod in thanks and then return my attention to Logan.

"I never saw an email. You should have called when I didn't reply to let you know I read it."

He holds his hands up.

"Yeah, I should have, but it's too late for that now. Your contract technically says I just have to give you notice."

The silence around us fills the air with tension.

"I'm just..." Ruby says quietly, jerking her thumb over her shoulder at her house and backing up. "I'll be back in a bit for Max. Oh, unless you want me to take him now? I'm sure you … actually, I don't know what you need right now. I mean, obviously a place to live, and you only have … you know, I think I'll just go."

I've never heard that woman ramble in my life.

I think I like it.

"Is that all you stopped by for?" My tone to Logan is anything but kind, and given the circumstances, I'd say it's fucking valid.

"Yep."

"Great. Goodbye, Logan."

"I really am sorry, Declan. I'll talk with you soon."

"Yeah, call this time," I say, and he waves with his back to me.

Fuck.

Two weeks to find a new place and move. Somewhere that doesn't require a lease, because we'll be moving into our own house in a few months.

I walk back into the house and freeze at the sounds of Susie and Max laughing.

Susie.

This is going to devastate her. I thought I had time to prepare her for the move across town.

Now I don't even know where we are going to live for the summer.

CHAPTER FIVE

RUBY

One of the things I missed the most when I was away from Lovers was Sunday breakfast with the family. Some families are fine with a peaceful, quiet breakfast, but I missed the chaos of these moments.

When Max and I used to visit, Luca and Miles made these mornings my son's favorite. Then Hudson moved home, and even though I know he struggled with Sundays in the beginning, I was still jealous of what I was missing. Of what Max was missing. But this right here, watching my brothers play with Max, this is everything.

"We're here!" the sweetest voice rings out at my front door.

I smile as she runs past me to the yard, and I roll my eyes at the man walking in behind her.

Even if he was on my mind all of last night after the run-in with his landlord.

His stress level must be at an all-time high. Oddly enough, I did a quick online search for houses for rent in town, but it was slim.

"No backyard gate today?" I force a smile as he steps into the kitchen.

"Good morning to you, too, Ruby."

"Everyone is outside."

He looks at his watch. "Dismissed in less than ten seconds. A new record."

I look over my shoulder slowly, replying with only a look that says go away.

"I'm going to miss these tender moments," his hand goes to his heart as he chuckles and walks out the door.

Miss them?

Oh, right, because he has to move to another part of town.

Bummer.

Shay passes him as she walks into the house, and I let out a breath.

"His face looks better today. I thought he'd have two black eyes this morning."

I laugh.

"I didn't hit him that hard. Just clearly in the right spot to make it look worse than it was."

Shay shakes her head. The moment the ball hit him, something inside me … changed. I had this urge to rush over and help him, and guilt hit me so hard I wanted to cry. That's not a feeling I'm used to when it comes to Declan, but I am human.

"So, do you think we can meet up this week sometime to go over the designs you have for The Marina?"

"Yes," I say with a giant smile, grateful for the change of subject. "I went a little overboard and stayed up late last night with a new idea."

I've always loved drawing and creating, really everything related to graphic design, and while romance book covers and social media graphics are my main source of income, having my friends or family ask me to make something for them has been a whole different kind of high.

Plus, the extra income has been nice.

Our friend Grace, whose family owns Lovers Lodge, asked me to make some for the lodge, too, and I've had so much fun letting my creativity run wild with new designs.

"Ruby, I only needed one new logo."

You know how some people can be looking at their phones and suddenly an hour or two has gone by while they just scroll through social media? That's how I am with design. I easily get swept away when I'm doing it.

"Fine. I won't show you the others."

She shoves my shoulder.

"You're showing me all of them," she says and then slouches against the counter. "I wish I were as gifted as you."

"Um, you own an entire marina. One that has taken a complete one-eighty from this time last year."

"I know."

My heart aches at how down she sounds.

I'd been gathering some plates and utensils to take outside, but I stop to give her my full attention.

"Hey, is everything okay?" I stand taller. "Are things with Luca okay?"

A goofy smile tugs at her lips.

"He's perfect, but don't tell him I said that. He already thinks he's this god because he … never mind."

I laugh. "Yeah, spare me the details, please."

I nudge her with my shoulder, and then, utensils in hand, we head out to the patio, where everyone else is seated.

Will I ever forgive myself for leaving them?

I know what I did was right at the time, but it doesn't make it any easier to know what I missed.

At some point, I need to move on.

I'm a different person now.

"I'm so hungry," Sadie says and digs in the moment all the food is out. Hudson is right there with her, passing the fruit bowl, and then like dominoes, everyone dishes up.

"Susie, Max, come get some food, please," Declan says. Both kids grab a banana and then run off to play again.

"It's better than nothing," I say, making my own plate.

"I agree. So, I don't really know if this calls for an announcement or anything," Declan begins, and everyone stops eating to focus on him. "But with the news that the house Susie and I are living in is being sold, we are moving back to my apartment in Chicago for the remainder of the summer until our house is ready."

Silence falls over the table, and I'm instantly flooded with happiness and dread.

Happiness that he will be far away from me and I won't have to listen to the town talk about him.

But dread for Max. He's so happy, and Susie plays a big role in that happiness.

Now she'll be leaving.

"I know Susie and I aren't actually part of the Asher family, and this is probably weird because everyone here is—"

"We consider you family, Declan," my father interrupts. "And this is unfortunate news. Luca, can you not move up the timeline for his house?"

"I looked into it last night when Dec called me. Between shipping dates on supplies, the schedule we have with plumbers and electricians, and my other jobs, I just can't see a way to do it that won't put my guys into a ton of overtime. It's summer. And it's hot. I can't do that to them."

"And I would never ask you to do anything that means people rearranging their entire schedule to accommodate me," Declan chimes in.

My eyes bounce around like pinballs as my brothers and Declan go over all the options. I don't know what to say. I just thought he'd be in another area of town and that was enough breathing space for me. But Chicago is a long way away. I doubt he'd plan trips back here just for the kids to play together before school starts.

"Any other rentals?" Miles asks.

"It would still be another thirty days before we could move in. Nothing is available sooner than that."

"Ruby has an entire unused basement," Luca adds quickly. "There are two rooms down there and a living room. It's—"

"Not your house to offer," I rush out before this choice is made for me.

Declan holds up his hands. "Like I said, I don't want to do anything that puts anyone out."

"And it would." My reply is laced with so much distaste, the entire table goes quiet.

"Ruby Ann Asher," my dad scolds. "What is wrong with you?"

Instead of answering, I stand quickly and head into the house.

I expect my dad or brothers to follow me but am pleasantly surprised when it's Shay, Quinn, and Sadie.

They all look at me with sad eyes.

"I didn't mean to sound so rude. I just, I barely know him and Luca just offers him my space."

"Barely know him? Ruby, you've talked to that man almost every single day for a year."

"Not by choice, and we mostly bicker."

"Bickering can be fun." Shay smiles.

"Not with Declan."

The girls all share a look.

"What's really going on?" Sadie asks.

"I … I don't know. I have my own space here, and until last year, I'd never had something that was just mine. I don't—"

"Don't want to give it up," Shay adds with an understanding nod.

"I get it, too," Quinn says. "And I'm not saying this because I think you should change your mind, but this is *your* house. Before, in Boston, it wasn't. Your house means your rules. Maybe set some and then charge him rent. Make it worth it for you."

"She has a point," Sadie agrees.

Me and Declan? Living in the same house? I can't even stand him when he's next door.

Not to mention what the town would say. They would probably find some way to turn this around so that he's making the sacrifice and not me. At the same time, if word gets out that my house was an option and I didn't offer it, they'd think I was unkind and the reason he moved away again.

I know it shouldn't matter what the town thinks of me, but damn it. I'm a good person, and I did the best with what I could when I was a seventeen-year-old girl.

And I could use that rent money right now.

A high-pitched squeal captures all our attention as Susie and Max jump on the trampoline, playing crack the egg.

I blow out a breath.

But sometimes in life, what I want isn't the only thing that matters.

CHAPTER SIX

DECLAN

By Wednesday, I've got movers scheduled, a cleaner lined up to get the condo ready in Chicago, and I've started packing. I'm still not thrilled over this outcome, but it makes the most sense.

What I haven't done is tell Susie.

The sooner I tell her, the better, but at the same time, telling her the day before we leave would leave less room for … I don't even know.

A fight? Fewer tears?

I'm her dad and should know the answer here, but my daughter loves to surprise me every chance she gets, and some days, I have no idea what I'm doing.

I park my truck outside Luca's house and get out.

Susie is with Max and Ruby for the next couple of hours while I enjoy boys' night.

The last one of the summer for me.

I knew this plan would suck for Susie, but to be honest, being back in Lovers has meant more to me than I thought. I wasn't a popular kid growing up, and I did have friends, but none of them treated me the way Ashers do.

The way the people of Lovers do.

The only positive is that I'll be closer to work and can give it more attention to get this deal over and done with.

Of course, it leaves me more room to easily fall into old habits I don't want, too.

I sure as hell hope the next few months go fast, and I don't just mean that for Susie.

The front door opens before I reach it.

"Tell me you changed your mind," Luca says.

"I wish, man."

I pass him and head to the living room. Everyone is already here.

Miles, Hudson, Dutton, and Linc, who is Sadie's brother and Hudson's best friend.

And all of them are looking at me.

"Oh-kay. What's going on?"

"Nothing." Hudson sighs. "We just think it sucks that you're leaving."

"I'll be back," I offer, but it doesn't help.

"You're still going to meet us in Vegas, right?" Luca asks.

I nod.

"Of course."

"I would quote you a price to stay at the lodge for the summer, but we're booked out into fall," Dutton offers. His family owns Lovers Lodge, the place this town is most known for.

"I'd say you could crash here," Luca says looking around the room at all the boxes, "but Shay just sold her place and is still unpacking, and the fact she's officially moved in excites me."

"Stop." Miles groans.

"What? I'm in love." Luca grins and sits.

"Hasn't she been living here since you two got engaged?" Dutton asks.

"Not officially, but yeah."

"What's the difference?" Linc asks.

"All her things are here now. Not just some of them," Luca answers without missing a beat.

"Fair point, and just so you know, I did check to see if any new rental listings showed up today. There weren't any."

"Thanks," I say to Linc. Given that he and his dad own the only real estate company in town, they would know if anything came up.

"Maybe we should talk to Ruby again," Luca says, but no one replies.

A timer from the kitchen dings, and Linc jumps up. "I'll get the pizza."

"Thanks. Look, I think it's safe to say your sister isn't going to change her mind. She was pretty clear on her feelings on Sunday, and that's okay. It's her house."

"Luca caught her by surprise. I'm sure if the idea was brought to her in a different way, she'd at least hear you out," Hudson says.

"She won't change her mind," Miles adds.

"I think she might," Luca argues.

I glance between Ruby's brothers. All three see a different side of her.

But no matter what they think she might or might not do, and no matter how hard I've tried to fix whatever I did wrong, Ruby Asher doesn't care much for me.

There is no way I can change her mind and convince her in less than a week to let me move in with her.

"Look, I really appreciate all the help and concern, but you'll barely notice I'm gone."

Linc walks in with the pizza cut into slices on a floral serving dish.

Everyone pauses and looks at Luca.

He chuckles.

"I told you that Shay has all her things here. Hence the flowers." He grabs a slice and then leans back. "So, who's ready for our first hoops game of the summer next week?"

"Are we ever ready?" Miles asks.

"I'd be more ready if we hadn't let Luca pick the team name." Dutton glares at him and takes a bite of his pizza.

"I'm sorry." Luca's voice is laced with sarcasm. "The Air Balls seemed fitting since we kind of suck."

"For who?" Hudson asks, and everyone laughs.

Yeah, I'll definitely miss nights like this.

———

THE FACT that I take the time to walk down my driveway, take the sidewalk in front of Ruby's yard, then turn up her driveway, all as her gaze tracks my every step from her seat on her front porch, is a dead giveaway that I'm avoiding something.

That something is telling Susie that we're going to move back to the city for the summer. If Luca stays on track, we can move into our new house just after Labor Day. So that's already a week shorter than expected.

Still, it's going to sound like a lifetime to my daughter.

I would ask Ruby if she's told Max, but I have the feeling she hasn't.

If she had told Max, he would have absolutely mentioned it to Susie by now. Those two talk nonstop when they are together.

"Do all boys' nights end with you frowning the way you are?" Ruby asks, her tone slightly teasing. I'm sure she intended an insult in that question somewhere, but I'm too distracted to find it right now.

With a sigh, I drop into a rocking chair on her porch.

"No, they don't. Tonight, however, I have to tell the number one girl in my life that we are moving for the summer."

I'm not sure why I just admitted that to Ruby. Our thing is snappy comments and heavy sarcasm with a side of an eye-roll. Not … deep front porch conversation.

Then again, Ruby is aware of my situation, and with our kids being besties and all, I'm sure she does have an interest in my choices.

She closes the book in her hand and flips it over, setting it next to her before she sits up straight.

"I actually wanted to talk to you about that."

My gaze shifts from the coverless book that she clearly took the wrap off to her eyes. Under the moonlight, there is a flicker of gold in them.

They're captivating in ways I could never admit to her.

Maybe this move would be good for me, too, in this sense.

I could finally stop thinking of her and treat her as just Max's mom.

"Yeah. Is it about how we're about to break the hearts of the two nicest kids in this town? How our summers are about to be filled with dramatics of how we ruined all their fun?"

Ruby's lips tug into a smile. It puts me off guard for a moment.

Making Ruby smile isn't something I do often.

"It's the opposite."

My brow lifts as I lean back and wait for her to go on.

"I …" She looks away, picking at something on the blanket covering her legs. "I thought it over, and the idea of you and Susie moving into the basement isn't … the … worst."

I rub under my nose to hide my smile.

I bet that was just as painful for her to admit as it was to hear coming off her lips.

"Is that so?"

"Mm-hmm."

"You were very against it when Luca brought it up."

"I was caught off guard, Declan."

I chuckle. There's my snappy Ruby.

"Well, that's very kind of you, but I don't want to impose, and telling Susie will be—"

"It would actually be doing me a favor, and I know you don't owe me any, but this is me extending an olive branch. I don't want to ruin Max's first full summer here just as much as you don't want to pull Susie away from this place."

"Yeah, but moving in together is a big deal."

"Only if we make it one."

I study her. The way she's relaxed into her seat, one leg crossed over the other, bare foot dangling in the air. Outside of the initial delivery of her offer, nothing about her posture right now suggests she's uncomfortable with this as she focuses on me.

"You're sure about this?"

She lets out a big sigh.

"I mean, it's a crazy idea, but it's not permanent and ..."

This time she looks away and starts to chew on her thumbnail.

"And ..." I prompt her.

Her hand drops, and she groans. "And I get the feeling you chose to move back here for a reason. As someone who made a similar choice, the idea of leaving again—"

"Makes you sick to your stomach?" I finish for her.

"Yeah."

I don't want to come off as too eager, but this offer, even coming from her, feels like a weight has been lifted off my shoulders.

And I haven't even given her my answer yet.

"I can't promise I'll be all roses and sunshine each day," she admits

"I wouldn't expect anything other than you being you, Ruby."

Her gaze narrows. "Right."

"You're really offering me an out?"

"I'm offering *myself* an out," she says without missing a beat.

I grin then stand up.

"Well, thank you."

"You're welcome."

I move to head into her house to grab Susie, but then stop.

"Hey, you know what?" I ask.

"What?"

"I bet that you and I are officially friends by the end of the summer."

She ignores me and opens her book.

"Maybe even best friends."

"Don't make me regret this."

I chuckle and head inside.

This summer just got a whole lot more interesting.

CHAPTER SEVEN

RUBY

I have regret.

Lots of it.

And it's been less than twenty-four hours.

I blow out my next breath.

There were so many things I should have said last night. Rules we should have set once he agreed to move in.

But this is Declan. Despite my feelings toward him, he's a grown man. My family trusts him, he will more than likely be okay with any rules I set, and I'm confident that this is all going to be fine.

It has to be.

I'm going to have to play nice.

I'm going to have to learn to relax.

I'm going to need advice.

The next girls' night couldn't have come at a better time.

Since I'm a little late, I park in front of Brooke's house and jog up the sidewalk. I don't bother knocking as I blaze through the door.

The girls are sitting in the living room with multiple trays of snacks on the coffee table and each of them with a mimosa in hand.

All eyes float to me in the doorway.

"I might have done something stupid," I say, finally closing the door, shrugging off my jacket, and joining the gathering.

Sure, I could have texted them about this all day long, but I needed to be face-to-face.

"Oh, this will be good," Brooke says, handing me her drink. "Take this. I'll make another."

I happily take the glass and sip as I try to process everything that's happened since last night.

Brooke returns from the kitchen, and guides me to a place to sit, since I'd just been standing in the middle of the room.

"Okay, go."

"I … wow, I never thought this would be something to come out of my mouth, but Declan is moving in with me."

A collective gasp fills the room.

"And Susie, of course."

"How did this … what did … are you two?" Brooke pauses to take a breath. "Did I miss something?"

My head jerks back like she slapped me. "What? No—God no. It's a long story."

"Good thing we have time." Grace grins and leans back, popping a piece of cheese into her mouth.

It takes me a moment to remember that neither of them were at Sunday breakfast.

"It's crazy, I know, but Logan is basically kicking him out of the rental."

"You used to want that. What changed?" Grace asks.

"Yeah, the other morning you were pretty dead set against this idea," Shay reminds me.

"Max and Susie changed that."

And the money idea, but I've never shared that part of my life with them, so they have no idea it's even a thing.

No one speaks, and I know they are waiting for me to elaborate. I know I shouldn't rearrange my entire life for my child's feelings, but I'd do anything for him and that includes letting the enemy move into my basement.

"It's not a secret that the friendship the two of them have formed has been amazing for Max. Turns out, Declan feels the same way for Susie." I shrug. "Neither of us wanted to let them down."

"Oh, that's cute. They truly are little besties, huh?" Tears form in Shay's eyes.

I nod. "I'm a little envious of it. I grew up without someone like that. I had friends, sure, but a best friend wasn't in the cards for me. Knowing I was taking that from him made me rethink everything. *So*, when Declan came home from boys' night last night, I offered the basement to him."

"And he was fine with it?" Quinn asks.

"He … would also do anything for his daughter, so yeah, he's in."

"I bet the kids were happy."

I smile, thinking about the hug Max gave me after I explained everything this morning. He has not stopped smiling since.

Then when I walked him to Declan's house before I came here, both kids immediately started planning movie nights every night.

That's obviously not happening *every* night, but there will be lots of them.

"Yeah, I can suck it up for him. It's only a few months."

"Couldn't Declan just buy a place for three months?" Sadie asks. "I know he mentioned looking for other places to rent, but buying a place wouldn't be out of the question, right?"

"That's a complete waste of money, even for one who has it." Grace smiles. "But I see what you mean."

The thought crossed my mind as well, but there is a reason he's smart with his money, and his financial choices are none of my business.

"Is he paying rent?" Brooke asks.

"Yes, he will be once I decide how much."

I figured that since I don't have a mortgage or rent myself, I'll just have him split bills with me and then add on an amount for wear and tear.

"Good."

Shay grins. "Soooo, you're doing something that a friend would do and helping him out."

"We are not friends." I tilt my drink to her. "Just enemies who now happen to be roommates."

"Eh," Sadie volleys her head. "Is it still enemies when you are the only one who thinks that?"

"Declan knows we are enemies."

"I think Declan has no idea why you don't like him and just goes with it so he doesn't piss you off more."

"And why don't you like him? Have you ever actually told us?" Grace asks.

I take another sip and then shrug. "I have my reasons."

"And they are …" Sadie encourages me to go on.

"I was always second-best to him in school while growing up, and then he moved back to Lovers the same week as me, which is weird in itself, but when he came back it was all, *oh, what a good dad and he's so successful and his daughter is so lucky because he's so amazing and oooh, he's so hot.* Blah, blah."

The girls just stare at me.

"So … you don't like him because everyone else loves him."

I grab a cracker from the tray and lean back.

"I mean, it's a little more than that."

"Okay …"

The room fills with silence again and I can't stand it.

"I've done things to be proud of, too." I toss my hands up in frustration. "I brought Max back here, and I have my business, and I'm … a good mom. I—"

"You're an amazing mom, Ruby," Shay cuts in. "I hope to be like you when it's my turn."

"Me too," Sadie says and reaches for my hand, squeezing it.

"I could never balance my life the way you do with a kid and a job. Alone. It's impressive," Brooke adds while Quinn and Grace nod.

"They're all right, Ruby."

"Well … I …" My eyes well with tears. "Thank you. I guess it's just nice to hear it. When we were in Boston, Colt's family constantly reminded me of the things I did wrong. I guess it's just nice to hear that I'm doing something right. Something good."

"Do the boys not say anything?" Quinn asks.

"My brothers?"

"Yes."

"No. I mean, they are busy, and they help me out so much as it is."

"Well, that's not okay. I'm going to—"

"No, no, please don't say anything to any of them," I say quickly, my gaze meeting Quinn's, Sadie's, and Shay's. "Please. I don't really talk about this stuff with them, so it would be weird for me."

"Do they know how Colt's family treated you?" Shay asks.

I shake my head. "I never talked about it because, despite all of it, I only really cared how Colt treated me, which was great. But it was still hard not to let the comments get to me. I was always doing my best, but it was never enough."

I shrug and then shake my head, standing to get a refill on

my drink. "But let's change the subject from my sad past to the bright future."

The girls all say *here, here*, and then Brooke adds, "to living with Declan."

And my smile drops.

Shit. I'd already forgotten that part.

CHAPTER EIGHT

DECLAN

Ruby may have agreed to let Susie and I move in for the summer, but I know her distaste for me wasn't cured overnight.

I grab a box from the kitchen and carry it out the front door, my mind scanning my memories to see if it can find what I did to her or to anyone close to her.

I definitely didn't date any of her friends. We are too far apart in age for that. Now, sure, a woman her age is fine to date, but as kids, no way.

That's out.

I wasn't in a feud with her brothers. Heck, we barely spoke in junior high or high school.

So that's out, too.

I jog down the steps, passing Luca and Miles, who are loading my couch into an enclosed trailer that I rented. They are arguing about how to place the furniture.

It's my shit, and I should probably stop to end the debate, but as long as it all fits, I don't care.

What I do care about is the fact that I'm moving Susie and

myself into a house with a woman who doesn't care for me all that much.

I know we are doing this for the kids, but I stand by my comment to become friends with Ruby by the end of the summer, and I feel like I should take this opportunity to mend things.

I grin as I approach her front door.

I don't think Ruby is going to make it easy for me.

And to be honest, I wouldn't expect anything else from her.

I kind of like that about her.

She doesn't give her affection, or whatever you want to call it, away easily. You have to earn it.

It might kill me in the end, but if Susie can learn even an ounce of that from Ruby, it would be awesome.

"Dad!" Susie greets me. "We are downstairs—my room is on the left, and yours is on the right."

I already know all this, but when the kids made it clear they wanted to be involved with moving day instead of playing in the backyard, Ruby gave them assignments.

Susie's role is to make sure that all the things are sorted into the right room.

"Perfect, but this box here is actually plates, cups, and silverware, so I'm headed to the kitchen."

She makes a waving motion with her arms. "Right this way! Please follow me."

I hear Ruby's laughter before we reach the space.

"I love how seriously you take your role, Susie."

"Well, Dad and I like an organized house, and he told me that living with you is probably like living with a drill ser—"

"This is great. I can take it from here, kid."

"Okay!" She bounces out of the room, stopping at the front door to wait for the next person.

"A drill sergeant?" Ruby asks, arms crossed and hip leaning onto the counter.

I slide the box onto the counter, ignoring her.

"It just occurred to me that moving my dishes here is pointless since your house is full of them. I'll go put this in the trailer."

"Smart."

I move to grab the bottle of water with my name on, courtesy of Max, whose job is to make sure no one becomes dehydrated.

But Ruby moves left at the same time.

"Oops."

Then right.

"Ah."

Then left again, as if we're in some sort of dance.

"Declan," Ruby snaps.

I grab her at the waist with both hands and hold her still. Then I move her in the opposite direction of my goal, but of course, Max chooses that same moment to race into the kitchen, announcing that he needs a new water for Luca. He bumps me from behind, forcing me to fall into Ruby.

I've now got her pinned between me and the counter, my front flush against her. The moment my chest brushes hers, I glance down.

She gasps and looks up.

My hands are still on her, and we freeze.

I know I should move, but the way her green eyes look up at me, the way they lock onto mine for the smallest of a second with not an ounce of distaste in them has me in a trance.

She takes a breath, and like me, doesn't move.

The tips of my fingers, the ones still holding her at the hips, tingle, and my heart pounds with a sickening feeling.

One that says if I don't dip my head and press my lips to hers, I'm going to regret it.

But that's crazy, right?

To have a feeling that consumes you this way.

To one moment be thinking of all the ways you can stay out of a person's space to suddenly never wanting to leave it.

I know I'm not the only one who feels it, because it's been a good thirty seconds and she hasn't told me to fuck off.

I sort of wish she would so that I can walk away and laugh at myself for even letting these thoughts entertain me.

But still … nothing.

Maybe … shit … does she want me to kiss her too?

As if she can read my mind, she nods slightly. It's so small that if I hadn't been giving my every piece of attention to her, I might have missed it.

My head barely moves before a throat clears behind us, breaking the spell.

She pushes me back so fast that I trip, but Miles reaches a hand out to assist.

"What's going on?" he asks, not a sliver of emotion on his face as he looks between me and his sister.

"Nothing," Ruby answers quickly.

A little too quickly, to be honest, but what do I know? I don't even know what to make out of what just happened with us.

I've never … that's never happened to me before.

I clear my throat. "Yeah, Max uh, he bumped me when he ran through the kitchen."

"Yep," Ruby says and walks out, leaving me alone with her brother.

He adjusts his stance, crosses his arms, and glares at me.

"Do you have something to tell me?"

"No."

"That was a fast answer."

"Because it's the truth."

He stares at me for another second, and I laugh. "Miles, it

was nothing. I bumped into her and we touched. It's nothing to worry about."

I grab the box of dishes that brought me into the kitchen in the first place and move for the door.

"Declan," Miles calls out. I pause and turn to face him.

"She's ..." His words trail off as he thinks them over. "Not like most women, alright. She's ..."

I nod. "I get it."

"I don't think you do. I'm not even sure what I'm trying to say."

I shrug. "I still get it, and like I said, you have nothing to worry about. Ruby and I are just friends. If that."

He nods and heads down the hallway.

As I walk down the porch steps and over the lawn to the trailer, his words play in my head.

She's not like most women.

He's absolutely right.

She's not.

If Ruby had it her way, I'd be living across town, farther from her right now, and yet ... I've never met a woman who made me feel the way I felt just now.

And I have no clue what I'm supposed to do about that.

CHAPTER NINE

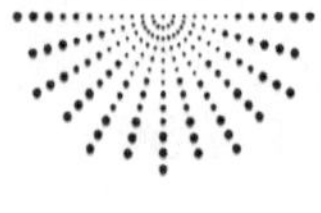

RUBY

I swing the door to B's Bakery open as if my life depended on it.

"Oh, we're closed. I'm sorry I forgot to switch the—Oh, hi, Ruby." Brooke beams when she sees us. "Can you flip that sign for me, Max?"

He nods and does as she asks.

"Thanks. If your mom says it's okay, I have some brownies left over today. Quinn is coming to grab them for Miles, but I bet he won't mind if you steal one."

"Nice." Max takes the treat from her.

"Can you find a table while I talk to Brooke really quickly?"

My son nods, and Brooke sneaks him a cookie to go with his brownie.

I find a spot farthest from Max, and Brooke meets me.

"I have not a clue what you want to talk to me about, but the fact you picked this spot where Max can't hear means it's good."

"It's … something." Declan's face moments before he was going to kiss me yesterday appears in my thoughts.

My stomach practically flips.

Flips.

Shit.

I lean forward

"Something happened yesterday when we were moving Declan and Susie into the house."

Brooke's eyes widen. "What happened? Oh my God, did his bed break and now you both have to share yours because, obviously, his giant body is way too large for your couch. Well, maybe not the one in the basement, but it probably still wouldn't be that … too much?"

I nod. "A little."

"Sorry. Okay, tell me the real story. I'll be quiet."

"We," I say even softer than before and glance at Max, "almost kissed."

"I can't hear you," she says and leans closer. "What?"

"We almost kissed."

"Look, Ruby, I understand you're trying to be quiet for the little ears nearby, but I can't hear you."

I roll my eyes and pull my phone out to text her.

Declan and I almost kissed.

Her phone pings, and then she slaps it to the table.

"What!"

"Shhh."

"What ... I mean, how did this happen?"

Now her eyes and smile are wide.

"This is not a smiling matter."

"Oh. Yes. It. Is."

"It just … we bumped into each other in the kitchen and then we didn't … separate until Miles walked in."

Brooke presses her lips together to keep from smiling, and her head does this odd bounce thing.

"Okay, okay. How do you feel about this?"

I palm my forehead.

"I think I wanted him to do it."

Now Brooke is making this weird squealing noise, but when I look up, she pulls herself together.

"I think …"

The door opens so suddenly, we both scream.

"Shoot, sorry," Grace says, and then Quinn walks in right behind her. "It says closed, but you didn't lock it. I saw Quinn, and she said you were expecting her."

"Yep." Brooke stands quickly, grabs the extra brownies, and hands them to Quinn.

"Hey, Ruby." She smiles.

"Hi." I look away quickly.

Now, even I know this isn't usual behavior for me and Quinn, so I'm not surprised in the slightest when she sits next to me.

"Is everything okay?"

I nod.

Then Grace sits.

"Are you sure?"

"Yep."

Silence falls over us, and then Brooke caves. "Declan almost kissed her," she whisper-shouts.

"Brooke." My gaze flashes to Max, whose head perks up.

"What?"

"Nothing. Are you ready?"

I jump to my feet, ready to make my escape, but I pause.

"Not a word of this to anyone, and that includes Miles," I tell my friends.

Quinn groans. "But this makes so much sense now. He came home all annoyed about Declan moving in."

"He did? Why?" I ask. They all like Declan. What would have changed his—oh.

"I asked, but he said it was nothing to worry about."

"It's not," I agree and then wave as Max and I head out the door.

"Can I go say hi to Uncle Huddy?"

"Yes."

I wait until he's heading off to Hudson's before I smile.

All these years later, he still calls him Uncle Huddy.

We enter through Sadie's bookstore, the one connected to Hudson's bar. Hudson excuses himself quickly from the couple he is talking to and makes a beeline for his nephew.

They do some fancy handshake that they made up last summer, and my heart swells.

It's the little moments like this that remind me why we came back.

As I wait for them to finish talking about the next time Max can go to hockey practice with Hudson, my gaze drifts out beyond the bar's seating area and to the floor-to-ceiling windows on the other side. Declan and Susie are walking down the street.

They get stopped by a woman who instantly laughs and then brushes her hand on Declan's chest. He steps back, nods to whatever she said, and then steps around her, but the woman keeps talking.

When he finally manages to escape, he turns onto Main Street, and within seconds he and Susie enter the bookstore.

"Max!" Susie hollers and then runs to her friend.

Declan walks in slowly, his hand stuffed into his pockets and his gaze on me.

After moving yesterday, he and Susie ordered pizza and kept to themselves in the basement, despite the kids' arguments.

It's for the best though. With the way he's looking at me right now, I'm not sure there wouldn't have been a repeat of what happened in the kitchen.

And that can't happen again.

From what I know, I have no doubts that Declan is a good man, but I learned my lesson about dating someone who has money, and I'm not about to repeat the past.

———

DECLAN AND SUSIE come up the stairs just as Max and I sit down to eat dinner.

"Oh, um, we …" he starts, but Susie just sits down at the table as if she's simply waiting for someone to put a plate down in front of her.

Declan's gaze flashes between her and me.

"Susie and I were just headed out to dinner. Come on, Susie."

"But they are having spaghetti and garlic bread, Dad. It smells so good. And" —she lowers her voice, facing her dad— "you know Ruby is a good cook—you talk about it all the time— so you know this is going to be super yummy."

I tilt my head to look at Declan, holding back my smile as I wait for him to reply.

He thinks I'm a good cook and talks about it with Susie. Words I'm sure he never wanted me to know but are nice to hear.

Declan clears his throat. "I …we …"

"Should sit down because it is good," Max says with a mouth full of noodles.

"Max," I scold.

"What?" He shrugs. "They live here now. They can't go out to eat every night just because we are using the table."

I nod, outsmarted by my child once again.

"He's right. Let me make you both a plate."

"I can do it," Declan says quickly. "Thank you."

"Yes!" The kids cheer at the same time.

"We should watch Mario again tonight after dinner," Max says to Susie, who nods eagerly.

"Well … that's—" I think over my words. It's night two. The kids are excited. A movie should be fine. Still. "We should make some ground rules," I say to Declan as soon as he sits down.

"I agree."

"How about after dinner, once we have the kids all set to go downstairs, we can make a list."

"Make a list," he repeats. "So organized."

My lips part to argue, but Max beats me to it.

"That's my mom. She loves a good list."

His smile is so proud.

My eyes meet Declan's for the smallest moment before he shovels a fork full of food into his mouth.

My gaze shifts slightly to his jaw and the way he chews. He's always had chiseled features with a slight shadow of a beard, but right now, his jawline is more pronounced than usual and his lips look plump and soft, and oh my gosh, I'm staring.

I look away quickly, focusing on my plate, stuffing my face, and listening to the kids talk about the different ways Bowser could have beaten Mario.

On my next bite, I look up once more.

My eyes find his like a magnet.

His lips tug to the right and then he winks.

"Dinner is delicious, Ruby. Thank you again for letting us join in."

I can feel my cheeks heat from the compliment.

"Yes, thank you," Susie adds with sauce all over her chin.

"Anytime. Maybe we can add dinners to the list."

"Only if you get to cook more nights than my dad," she says in a whisper.

Declan doesn't even try to look offended. He just grins and says, "I second that vote. Your cooking is way better than mine."

I smirk but look down so he can't see it, and continue eating.

Better than him.

It has a nice ring to it.

The rest of the dinner goes with ease, and I hate to admit that I actually enjoy the company.

As soon as we are finished. Declan takes Susie downstairs to change into her pajamas and start a movie.

Max also changes and then sprints to the basement.

I finish cleaning the kitchen, a much shorter argument between Declan and I this time, and then I settle in the living room upstairs to wait for him. The creak in the stairs is my only hint that Declan is on his way.

As soon as he reaches the top step, my heart begins to race.

Oh-kay.

Gray sweatpants. Black T-shirt. Backward ball cap. Black rimmed glasses.

It seems Susie wasn't the only one who went downstairs to change into their sleepwear.

This man needs to go right back down those stairs and change every single thing he has going on.

But of course, I can't tell him that.

I just need to take a deep breath and pretend like it doesn't bother me.

"I brought a notebook just in case you wanted me to write this down."

Damn him.

His ability to read me shouldn't turn me on.

"Thank you," I say and then sit down on the chair across from him, tucking my legs to sit crisscross applesauce. "Where should we start?"

He tilts his head, his brows rising for a split second. "I'm good with wherever you pick."

"Okay, well, let's just start from the beginning of the day. You obviously have bathrooms in the basement to get ready, so we can cross that off."

"Bathrooms crossed off, check," he says, never taking his eyes off me.

I narrow my gaze, "Breakfast is … pretty much anytime Max wakes up. I work from home, so we aren't rushed to be ready by a certain time during the summer."

"Same with me and Susie."

My gaze snaps to his.

"So, wait, we're just here all day every day … together?"

I knew Declan still worked and obviously from his house, but the details didn't register when I invited the Youngs to move in.

"Seems so. Let's make this easier. For breakfast and lunch we obviously leave for each family to do their own thing when they see fit. Susie and I usually go out to dinner once a week, but I can make that more often while we are here if I need to."

"No, no, I don't want you to feel like you can't be here, but there is only one kitchen."

"So …."

"So how about we agree to three dinners a week together … for the kids' sake."

Declan leans back and chuckles, "Yes, for the kids' sake. I hope you can survive that."

I hold my chin high as I say, "If they are like tonight, I can survive and —no, stop. Don't smile."

"I can't help it. I think we're friends and you just refuse to admit it."

I refuse to have a reply.

He laughs. "Well then, let's move on to rent."

I nod slowly.

"I don't really know where to start on that. It's only three months."

I hate how unsure I sound, but I truly feel that something like this should be discussed together. I never had that option before, and I'd hate to take it from anyone else.

"How about I pay you two thousand a month or six grand up front?" he suggests with a simple shrug.

I ...

He...

What?

This is so typical for someone with money. To just act like it means nothing, like it's not a big deal.

It is a big deal and completely insulting.

Does he think I can't afford this place?

I'm half tempted to tell him to fuck off and I'll just cover the bills to prove a point, but fuck ... the whole point was to get extra money, and as much as I'd love an extra two grand a month, that number makes me feel like I'm a charity instead of someone helping out someone else.

I could start an argument, but this is the start of a long summer.

"How about one thousand a month?"

He jerks his head back, and this time, it's as if he's the one who is insulted.

"Two seems more fitting."

"Why?"

"Because I've looked at the market in this area, and that's the number that fits. Not to mention we'll double the water bill, my daughter will leave every single light on, and I'll want the AC on all night every night. Add in the extra feet running up and down the carpet stairs and you'll need that cleaned when we leave, and more down downstairs. The dishwasher will run twice as much, and the—"

"Fine." I hold my hand up to stop him. He's clearly thought about this. "Fifteen hundred and we leave it at that."

"But ..."

"Please, Declan, just agree with me."

He pauses, gaze locked on mine for a beat before he nods.

"Alright. This is your house. What you say goes."

I blow out a breath and look away. Only when I look back, his eyes are still focused on me.

It only increases my awareness of him. Of how it feels like he is trying to read my mind. As if he's trying to understand me in a way no one ever has.

"What topic is next?"

His question eases the tension in my shoulders, and my breath returns to normal.

"Food. Kids are kids, and if I buy something that Susie wants to eat, let her. Even if she finishes it."

"Same rules for me with Max."

"Thank you."

"Is there anything Max can't eat? I would assume I'd know this by now, but he's not with me full time."

"He's good. Susie?"

"She's good too."

"Next?" I ask.

"I do have a topic, but it's a little off from all this. What about Max's dad?"

"Colter? What about him?"

"Does he know that I'm living here?"

I'd called him before I had the conversation with Declan on the patio. He was comfortable with whatever decision I made.

"He's fine with it."

"Just like that?"

"Yes. Colt and I have a good relationship. He trusts me and I trust him. He's a great guy. Not the guy for me, but he's a good man. And Susie's mom?"

He doesn't even look up. "Gave up her right to have an

opinion years ago when she told me she didn't want to be a mother anymore."

My heart instantly aches for him. For Susie. I hear the pain of what that means. Of the new light this news sheds on the kind of man Declan is.

There are so many things I want to say.

How could she?

What kind of mom doesn't want to be in their child's life?

Why did she leave?

But instead I say, "Her loss."

He glances up. "Yeah. It is."

The silence falls between us, so painful that my next sentence comes out before I can think twice about it.

"Since the kids have taken over the basement, I guess you can stay up here to watch a movie with me if you want."

I reach for the remote and turn on the TV.

"Thanks, but I have some emails to go over, so I'm going to head back down."

"Oh. Okay, yeah."

He stands. "Let me know if we need to talk about anything else."

"Okay."

"Night, Ruby."

"Good night, Declan."

He heads back down the stairs and I watch his every step.

I invited him to hang out with me, and he said no.

I should be happy.

But I'm not.

CHAPTER TEN

DECLAN

Setting the rules last night was a good idea.

It was something we should have thought about doing before Susie and I actually moved in, but as we discussed, there are going to be a handful of moments when we need to make a ruling as they arise.

I jog up the stairs, the image of Ruby in her pajamas last night still on my mind.

It was a random pair of sleep shorts and a short-sleeved T-shirt. They weren't even matching. They weren't revealing. I mean, sure, the shorts were short and maybe if she moved in a certain way I'd have seen more, but everything about it was pretty modest. Which turned me on even more. She revealed just enough to tease.

The part that turns me on the most is the fact that she doesn't even know how beautiful she is.

She's smart, creative, and loves her kid with all her heart.

I guess there are a lot of things about Ruby Asher that turn me on.

And then she invited me to watch a movie with her.

Innocent. Everything about it, yet my mind instantly went to how I haven't done something that mundane with a woman in more than a year. Maybe even two.

And I wanted to. In fact, I want to—

"You're kidding me, right?"

I spin from making coffee to see the woman who has been on my mind all night long glaring at me, her arms crossed, hip cocked to the side, and a scowl on her face. She's wearing the same pajamas she had on last night, but now they are wrinkled. Thoughts of her lying in bed cross my mind.

I don't need more images of her in my mind.

As her eyes take me in, the scowl morphs from annoyed to … hungry.

Fuck. This does it for me, too.

"Are you just going to stand there like"—she gestures up and down my body—"that?"

I glance down at my sweats and bare feet. I flip my ball cap backward and match her stance, only I'm leaning on the counter.

"You're going to have to be more specific. I'm a smart man, Ruby Asher, but it seems I have no idea what's going on when it comes to you."

I've never spoken truer words.

"Gross, is that a pickup line?"

"A pickup line?" I repeat. "This proves my point. I have no idea what's going on right now."

She huffs and marches into the kitchen, nudging me with her hip, so she can take over making the coffee.

"What's going on is, you seem to enjoy walking around in nothing but a pair of sweats. I never said anything when we were at your house or in your space, but this is two mornings in a row."

She's counting?

"I have a hat on."

"I'm aware."

"Sooo, the problem is …"

"You need a shirt if you're going to be standing in my kitchen."

"Oh, is that a rule we made last night and I forgot?"

"It's a rule I made just now because I didn't know that I needed to make it a rule last night."

I grin as her gaze slips to my pecs, pausing just long enough for me to catch it.

"Is this a new rule because I'm actually shirtless or because you can't seem to stop sneaking a look at my naked chest?"

She sighs, and even though I know it shouldn't, it makes me smile.

"I'll go put a shirt on, but save me some coffee."

"Thank you."

I jog down the stairs to retrieve a shirt and then return to the kitchen to find Max at the kitchen island, eating a bowl of cereal shirtless.

Alright. Alright. So she had a good point.

"Morning, Dec," he grins.

"Morning, Maxwell." I ruffle his hair. "Where did your mom go?"

"Um, she said she needed a cold shower."

"Did she now?" I pour myself a cup of coffee and then make myself a bowl of cereal. We eat in silence until Susie comes up the stairs.

"Oh wow," Max says, his eyes wide.

My daughter's hair is a wild mess. I do not doubt that there are tangles in it. It's a normal sight for me, but I understand the shock on his face.

When she was younger, she wore a ponytail every single day for a year. Maybe more. Any other hairstyle was a fight that I tried to avoid every morning, so the quickest style I knew how to do was a simple ponytail.

Brushing a young girl's hair is an experience all on its own.

Thankfully, she manages it mostly on her own now.

"What?" Susie asks, grabbing the box of cereal and sitting next to him. She reaches her hand into the box and pulls out a handful.

"A bowl, Susie, please," I say, and she rolls her eyes before getting up to get one.

"Your hair," Max says and then looks at me. "Is it always like that?"

"In the morning, yes."

"Don't be mean," Susie says just as Ruby walks back into the kitchen. Her hair is pulled into a messy bun on her head, and she is wearing makeup.

That was a quick shower.

"Can you do my hair like yours?" Susie asks. Ruby pauses.

"Oh, um, I've never done someone else's hair before."

"What about Max's?"

Ruby pours her coffee. "His hair is short and easy to style."

"Oh, okay."

Susie's shoulders drop, and she hangs her head.

Ruby looks at me.

I mouth *it's okay*, but I can see in her eyes that's not enough.

"Can I watch a YouTube video or something first?" My daughter's face lights up as she nods.

"Dad, show her the ones you like."

Ruby's little side smile makes my heart skip a little.

I like it when Ruby smiles at me.

It makes me feel like I did something right, and that's a rare moment in her eyes.

"I'll text you a couple of links," I say.

"I'll go change while you look at them," Susie announces and races down the steps.

My phone alerts me just then.

Shit. I forgot I had this call this morning. I meant to get Susie up earlier to be ready to go to the library where I could work and she could play or take her tablet as backup. I was clearly distracted.

"Is everything okay?" Ruby asks.

I hold up my phone.

"With all the changes in the last week, I forgot about a Zoom meeting I have in thirty minutes. It's probably going to take an hour or two."

Ruby doesn't miss a beat.

"What does Susie do when you're working?"

"If she is not with Max, she's watching TV. Sometimes we go to the coffee shop or the library and she colors or—"

"What if she came with me and Max today? We are just going to be out for a couple of errands and then to The Marina to hang out with Shay on the beach around lunch. We debated hiking the trails at one point, too. She's more than welcome to join us."

Her offer cuts off my train of thought.

"You want to watch my daughter while I work?"

She waves a hand in front of her face. "Oh, please. Once these two get going, it's hardly watching anyone. They entertain each other."

She's right, but still, that was not my intention with this arrangement at all. But the temptation of all the work I could get done knowing Susie is taken care of and having fun is big.

"I ... I didn't move in here for you to become my babysitter."

"I know," she says before I can say more. "But I know what it's like to juggle a work-from-home job and a kid all on your own. Take it while you can."

"I'd love to, but it's boys' night, too, and I would feel awful asking someone to watch her for this and then ask someone else again for tonight. It's—"

"Fine with me. I'm here anyway, Declan. Relax."

My phone buzzes again—my lead manager back in Chicago reminding me of the meeting and asking whether I have the reports he sent me.

"Okay, yeah. If you're positive."

"We are," Max answers for her and then pushes away from the table. "Susie!" he yells as he races down the stairs.

"You might have your hands full today," I say and stand up.

"I'll manage."

"Well, thank you."

She nods.

I rinse my bowl out and place it in the dishwasher, glancing over my schedule. She's watching me.

I don't comment on it though. She's doing me a favor, and I'm not about to rock that boat, but a part of me is going to wonder all day long what's going through her mind.

And as much as I want to know, I do know how lucky I am right now.

The sooner I prepare for this meeting, the sooner it will go and if I'm lucky, the closer I'll be to owning Collins Corp.

———

MY MEETING LASTS THREE HOURS.

Three.

Hours.

I come upstairs to see what Susie is doing, but the house is empty. Only a note from Ruby that says they left, about an hour before my meeting was over, and that they will be gone for a few hours. Leave it to Ruby to leave a note instead of texting me.

She despises texting me.

That gives me two full hours with nothing on my plate.

I start by cleaning the dishes in the sink and placing them in the dishwasher. Then I wipe the counters down. Then I vacuum.

That takes up a whole hour of my time, so I make a sandwich for lunch and head back to the basement to see what I can clean there.

It isn't much. Ruby keeps things clean.

So I settle for more work until I hear the patter of feet upstairs a couple of hours later.

I race up the steps to find my daughter.

I crave time for myself, but the moment I get it, I wish she were here with me.

"Dad!" Susie calls out and runs to hug me.

I beam, hugging her back.

"Wow," I say. "Look at your hair."

"Isn't it the best? I think Ruby just replaced you as the one who does my hair."

"Well," I say, "we can take turns. I mean, if she's up for it."

Ruby is smiling, so that's a good sign.

"It was just two French braids down the sides, nothing fancy."

"Nothing fancy," I repeat. "There are hardly any stray pieces falling around her face, giving her that wild child look."

Ruby laughs.

"I had a paste, and it seemed to work."

"I need to know what it is so we can buy some."

"I'll go get it!" Max cheers and runs up the stairs.

Susie follows him.

After they are out of sight, Ruby turns to me. Her skin is sun-kissed, and her smile is contagious. "I'm sorry we were later than my note said. The kids were having so much fun, and I didn't want to ruin it by making them come home."

"It's fine. It looks like she had a good time."

"She did. I have pictures I can text you later."

"Great."

"When do you leave for boys' night?"

"Just under two hours. Do you want me to cancel?" I ask without hesitation. She's had Susie all day.

"Nooooo," Susie says as she comes down the stairs. "You can't cancel boys' night. We have plans, Dad."

I hold my hands up.

"Oh, sorry. I wasn't aware."

Ruby laughs at my exaggerated response, and I would laugh with her, but my daughter is now looking up at Ruby, her eyes shining.

And Ruby smiles back.

Now, I've seen them smile before, but this moment feels different.

There is a pause that … shit.

It hits me in the chest all too fast, and I have to clear my throat to pull myself together.

I've never seen Susie look at someone like that.

Like she trusts her just as much as she trusts me. The noise I make has everyone looking at me now.

"Well, how about I take these two out back for a quick game of soccer before I go."

"Or," Max says quickly, "we can play two against two."

"Girls versus boys!" Susie says and sprints outside. Max follows her.

"I wish I had their energy," Ruby says, walking into the kitchen and pouring a glass of water.

"I was attempting to give you a break. I can tell them it's just me if you want."

"Why?" she replies instantly. "Afraid you'll lose?"

I chuckle and toss my head back.

"No."

She places her lips on the glass and drinks.

Nothing about it should even faze me. People drink water every single day, and I've never thought twice about it.

But right now, I'm watching the way her eyes close, her head tilts slightly back, and her throat bobs with each gulp.

I step forward. I need to be near her.

She sets the cup down and looks at me.

"Are you ready?" She walks past me and out the door.

Ready for this game, yes.

Ready to keep myself under control while living with Ruby? I'm about to find out, because if the look on my daughter's face said anything just now, it's that whatever kind of relationship I choose to have with Ruby, I better not fuck it up.

"WHY ARE YOU LIMPING?" Luca asks.

I managed to sneak into his house and get through most of the evening without anyone noticing, but now that I'm getting up for another slice of pizza, I can't hide it.

"Soccer mishap," I answer, keeping it short.

"Susie?" Miles asks.

I shake my head.

"Max?" Hudson asks.

I shake my head again.

The Asher brothers share a look, then Luca laughs and asks, "Ruby?"

I nod.

"How?"

"We were playing a little two on two-on-two in the backyard before I came here. We were battling at the net, and she kicked my shin a lot harder than I would expect her to kick a ball."

Luca doubles over in laughter while Hudson shakes his head.

Miles just stares at me. "How is that going, by the way?" he asks.

I grab another slice of pizza from the box on the table and return to my seat.

"Good. It's only been a couple of days, but good."

"I saw them at the beach today. Ruby, Max, and Susie," Luca says. "They looked like they were having fun. She said you were working. That sucks."

I nod and open my mouth to reply, but Miles beats me to it.

"Don't take advantage of her."

Dutton and Linc had been discussing real estate, but now their attention is on Miles and Me.

"I'm not."

"Then why—"

"Miles, chill," Luca cuts him off. "Ruby plans to take advantage of him, too."

Miles's eyes widen.

"Not that way, no. I'll definitely be watching Max for her too. She needs a break as much as I do, and I'll be happy to help her."

The air in the room feels heavy.

I've always gotten along with the Ashers, but it feels like as of late, Miles has a new opinion of me. I don't enjoy it.

I didn't do anything wrong, and I'm not about to sit here and argue with him.

She's his sister and he has every right to be protective of her. I just need to find a way to show him that he doesn't have to worry when it comes to me.

"Speaking of"—I grab my pizza and stand back up—"I should get going."

Luca stands to see me out, but he smacks Miles on the back of the head on the way.

"Sorry about him. He's … weird lately."

"It's fine. If I had a sister, I'd be the protective brother, too. I just wish he knew he doesn't have to do that with me."

"You're a guy and you live with our sister. We're programmed to be wary, especially with you."

I laugh.

"I trust you, if it helps." Luca grins.

"It does. Thanks."

I limp to my truck and drive the short distance to Ruby's house.

As soon as I walk in the house, I freeze.

I didn't expect the kids to be asleep quite yet, but I definitely didn't expect to see all three of them in the upstairs living room with *Despicable Me* on the TV, feet up and their faces covered in what looks like wet paper.

Not a single one of them turns to look at me.

"We just put one on, Dad. Do you want one?" Susie says. At least she knows I'm here.

Ruby laughs. She clearly thinks I'm going to say no.

Little does she know, I'm well versed in the life of a girl dad who's single.

"I would love one. I've had a long day, and although I'm very thankful for Ruby, I could use the extra relaxation."

"Well, come sit here," Susie says, making me a spot next to Ruby on the couch.

She tears the package open and holds up a white mask that looks slimy as fuck.

"Lay back," she says, pressing my head into the back of the couch, and lays the mask on my face.

It's colder than I thought.

"You have to put your feet up," Max says from his chair. "Really get the whole effect of a spa day at home."

"Spa day? You've been doing this all night?"

"Yep! I told Ruby how you do the masks with me, but then she suggested painting our nails and toes, too. It's been the best."

More and more details of their entire day spill from my daughter's lips, but my eyes remain on Ruby.

She meets my gaze, and my heart beat takes off.

Is it racing because I'm attracted to her, or because of the joy she's given my daughter in just one day?

Shit.

I relax with my face mask, and within a half hour, both kids are fast asleep.

I pick up Susie and take her down the stairs, then I return to help Ruby clean up their spa day.

Max has gone to bed as well, and Ruby is scrubbing something on the chair.

"Everything okay?"

She looks over her shoulder.

"I knocked over Max's chocolate milk," she says. The entire seat of the cloth recliner is soaked.

"Looks like you got it," I tell her as she gathers the cleaning supplies and passes me on her way into the kitchen.

"I think so, too, but you'll have to sit on the couch."

"For?" Did we need to add something to the rules?

"A movie."

"Oh, are we watching one?"

Her eyes go wide. "No, no, I mean, I am, and I thought you came back up because maybe you'd want to watch something that wasn't a kid movie, but it's fine. I mean, you do have a TV downstairs. I shouldn't have—"

"A movie sounds good."

She disposes of the cleaning supplies and returns to the couch where we sit together and agree to watch *Happy Gilmore*.

About ten minutes into the movie, Ruby finally shifts from

placing her feet flat on the ground to tucking her bent legs to the side.

I'm suddenly aware of how close she is and how, in a short amount of time, I have become less of an enemy in her eyes.

It's exactly what I wanted and is in no way a reason for my mind to wonder how I want to touch her right now, even if it's just shoulder-to-shoulder contact.

I clear my throat.

"Need anything to drink?" I ask her.

"Oh, maybe just water."

"You got it."

I make two glasses of ice water and return.

Only this time I sit down closer to her.

So fucking close that our arms touch.

And get this.

She doesn't even flinch.

Fuck.

Why am I suddenly nervous?

This is Ruby.

I know her.

Happy is doing his thing on the screen and Ruby is cool as a cucumber and I'm not. I'm sitting here trying to talk myself out of hitting on her.

Her brother clearly doesn't trust me now that I live here and Susie is getting attached.

Both are valid reasons why this should not be a thing.

She reaches her arm across her body, and I flinch.

She looks at me.

"Are you good?"

"Yep."

She grabs the blanket she keeps over the arm of the sofa and covers her body.

"Are you cold?" she asks.

I'm fucking sweating, Ruby.

"A little," I say, and she extends the blanket.

What am I doing?

Is this high school?

Am I just going to slip my hand under the blanket and finger her as if we have to hide it from our parents?

Shit.

I need to go downstairs.

Now.

Ruby rearranges her position once more, and this time, her legs drop to rest on mine.

"Oh, sorry," she says and starts to move again.

"It's okay." I put my hands on her legs to stop her. "You had a busy day. If this is relaxing for you, do it."

Her eyes meet mine for a beat too long before she looks at the TV again.

She shifts again and takes a deep breath.

My thumb instinctively starts to rub back and forth on the bare skin of her calf. She doesn't tell me to stop, so I add a little pressure, and she moans.

It's soft, and if I hadn't been in tune with her, I would have missed it.

Still, the sound makes my cock jump, and I close my eyes, but I don't stop rubbing her legs.

After a moment, she stretches her legs out, placing one on top of the other, and grins at me.

"You can't just do one leg."

I let out a chuckle and start massaging the other leg.

Every now and then, she makes a little noise, and it only makes me harder. Sexual or not, it turns me on to make her feel this good.

Suddenly, she sits up, grabs her water, and starts chugging.

"I should go to bed," she says and then stands. She turns to step over my legs, which are propped up on the table, but she gets snagged on the blanket and falls into my lap with one leg on either side of mine.

I grip her hips to steady her before she lands on my erection, but I'm not fast enough.

Her eyes go wide when she feels me.

My heart pounds. I'm pretty sure I just fucked up this arrangement. She's clearly about to run. An apology springs to my lips.

But then she sits on me.

Her warm core pressed right against my cock.

Her eyes close, and I finally let myself breathe.

Her hands come to rest on my shoulders, but other than that, she doesn't move.

She doesn't say a word and neither do I, but she grinds into me, and one of her hands strokes up my face, cups my cheek.

I keep my hands at her sides and guide her.

I grow harder each time she rocks her body and with each pant she lets out in my ear.

"Dad, are you up here?" Susie's voice sails up the stairs, and Ruby leaps off me.

"Yeah, honey, what's wrong?" I say, marching for the steps to tend to my daughter.

She rushes into my arms, and as I retreat down the steps to put her back to sleep, I glance at the stairs that lead to Ruby's room.

She's gone.

CHAPTER ELEVEN

RUBY

I have officially done Susie's hair every single day now for a week.

I'd say I'm swiftly approaching advanced status. I have no idea why Declan thinks it's so hard.

I hate to admit it, but having Declan here this past week has been helpful. Not only has he watched Max so I could get some work done, but he has different ideas on play than I do, and there has been no shortage of fun for the kids.

The only downside has been that Declan is now in my space every day of the week, and it has made it very, *very* hard to avoid him after what happened on the couch the other night.

God, it was so good.

But it was wrong for so many reasons. For starters, it was impulsive, and it goes against every thought I'd told myself. As if I'm levelheaded when I'm alone, but the minute we are close to touching, my brain suddenly glitches and all the warning signals shut off.

Either way, it can't happen again. I have no doubt that he agrees and that is why he hasn't mentioned it either.

I *can't* touch him.

Not again.

Everything about this situation is complicated.

I can't remember the last time I was that turned on by anyone, and he barely touched me. He didn't even kiss me. We only rubbed against each other and didn't even get to finish. Which is exactly why it can't happen again.

It.

Won't.

I need to focus on work and how, even though I can make double loan payments for a few months, I still need to keep up my clientele if I want to continue doing so after they move out. What I don't need to focus on is what the man living in my basement looks like naked.

Today was a busy one keeping the kids entertained, and even though there were moments I could check my emails and make quick replies, I still have a lot of work to do tonight.

With Max finally settled in with a movie, I grab my laptop and sit on the couch with the mouse resting on the sofa arm. It's the best makeshift mouse pad a girl could ask for. I open my email first and check a few things to make sure I'm on schedule. Then I open my Notes app to see what's next for the day.

As soon as I double-click on the file for the graphics I need to work on, my entire computer screen goes black.

No. No, no, no.

This can't be happening. I just got a new computer last year. I should still have a few more years before it does this to me.

I groan and press a couple of keys, hoping that it's going to wake up my computer, bringing it back to life.

I tap the enter key again and again, then harder. *Please just blink.* Anything. A cursor or a note to tell me that I need to fix this. I'll take anything at this point.

Ten return taps later and still nothing is happening.

This is just my luck. First, my entire life is thrown off its routine, but the one thing I do have control over is work and my computer crashes. Life couldn't get any worse.

I let out the loudest groan of all time.

"Everything all right?"

Declan is at the top of the stairs. White shirt, backward black hat, and a pair of gray sweatpants.

My eyes drift down to see if the rumors are true about what they say. Yep, right there in front of me is an outline of the very thing I should not be thinking about.

I take a deep breath.

I stand corrected. Things can get worse.

"Everything is fine, thank you very much."

"Really? Because the noise that came out of you just gave me the complete opposite vibe."

"I didn't make any kind of noise, and noises don't give vibes."

Even with my back to him, I sense him walking toward me. On the one hand, he's the perfect person to have near when something like this happens, but on the other hand, that means accepting his help would result in us being up here together. Alone.

Not a good plan for me.

"It would help if you turned your computer on."

"Ever the smart one, aren't you?"

Yes, be snappy. Make him mad. Then maybe you won't be so attracted to him.

Because the couch that I'm sitting on is facing the living room front window, I can see his reflection. He leans forward, resting both hands on the back of the couch, one on either side of my shoulders, and then he slowly leans forward. "Looks to me like someone's having computer trouble."

"I don't need your help."

"It sort of looks like you do."

"Just because it looks like I need it doesn't mean I want it."

For heaven's sake. Listen to me arguing just to argue so that we aren't the only two in a room. I clearly need his help.

"Is there a reason you came upstairs?"

Whatever he came up here for, I need him to just move along and grab it and return to the basement so that I can be depressed and sex-deprived in private. Then I can make a plan to fix my computer.

"The kids want popcorn."

I stand quickly and head into the kitchen. Declan is right behind me, watching my every move. I'm sure that by now he knows where the popcorn is in this house. Max is addicted to it; he has it at least twice a week when he's watching a movie before bed.

It's a habit I'll break on another day.

I grab one of the bags from the cabinet and jam it into Declan's chest.

"Here."

He lets out the lightest grunt.

I head back to the living room.

"Why don't you just let me make this popcorn, take it to the kids, and then I can come back up here and help you?"

"Because I told you that I don't want your help."

And we do not need to be alone.

"Ruby, it's obvious your computer isn't working. I can fix it."

I ignore him and attempt to turn my laptop on once more.

Nothing happens.

The popcorn starts to pop in the microwave as I weigh my options.

One, ask around to Lovers to find out who the tech guy everyone calls for help. Get on his schedule, cross my fingers that he knows how to fix whatever this is within days, and then pay him. Two, wait until this weekend and drive to one of the two computer stores in Wind Valley. It'll cost more, and I should definitely call ahead to be sure they can get me in. Three, ask the man in my kitchen to help me, and possibly have this fixed tonight so that I can get some work done.

And maybe sit far enough away from him while he works.

I can totally do that.

The microwave beeps and I hear Declan pour the snack into two bowls.

I hug my computer to my chest and stare at him.

He's at the top of the stairs when he sees me.

"Can you please help me?"

He smirks as he starts the descent to the basement. "I'll be right back."

I grab a water and then jog up the stairs for my computer bag. I don't see him needing the charger for anything, but I'll have it ready. When I get back to the living room, Declan is just hitting the top step. He's got two new things with him: a bag with his company logo on it, and he's also wearing my new weakness, his black rimmed glasses.

Damnit. I'm a mess.

"What were you doing when it turned off?"

"Working."

He grabs my computer from the coffee table and moves to the kitchen table. I join him. Two chairs down.

"I need you to be more specific."

"I was opening a file jand I'm not a professional or anything, but normally, that mundane action shouldn't cause a computer to shut down."

"I agree."

He gets to work, somehow pulling up a screen that reminds me of a really old video game and typing in code.

"Are you going to watch me the entire time?"

I sigh and lean back.

"I'm just worried that I won't get my files back."

"Do you back them up?"

"I think just to the cloud or whatever comes with Apple."

"We have other ways to access them if your computer is done for good."

His fingers fly over the keyboard, and he keeps working.

Silence falls over us, so I send a text to the girls in the group. Maybe if I talk this out, I can stop internally obsessing and move on. I better go ahead and skip the small talk.

RUBY:

So, last week I pretty much gave Declan a lap dance.

GRACE:

I LOVE how you never beat around the bush with anything.

SHAY:

What!

SADIE:

O M G.

BROOKE:

I thought you didn't like him.

RUBY:

I don't … or didn't. I don't know. Things lately have been quiet, and he's … not that bad.

QUINN:

Group girls' chats are my favorite.

RUBY:

The point is, I don't know how to act now.

BROOKE:

What do you mean? Have you not talked
about it? Is he a good kisser?

RUBY:

We never even kissed! I just dry humped him
until his daughter interrupted and ran to my
room.

SADIE:

What does this mean?

RUBY:

Nothing. I slipped up. I'm attracted to him,
yes, but that doesn't mean anything needs to
happen.

SHAY:

Sometimes it does, though.

I sigh and set my phone down. This chat isn't as effective as I
needed it to be. Then my phone vibrates, and I pick it up again.

GRACE:

If you don't know what it means, just don't
stress. Do nothing.

I let out a light laugh. As if it were that easy. Declan's gaze
flickers to mine for a split moment. I go back to texting so that I
don't stare at him.

RUBY:

Did you know he wears glasses at night?

GRACE:

I did not.

RUBY:

Thick black-rimmed ones.

QUINN:

And you're telling us the details because?

RUBY:

I think I have a thing for men in glasses.

GRACE:

A guy thing or a Declan thing?

I STARE AT MY PHONE, debating whether I should tell them how I really feel about the couch night. I bite my lip as I weigh my options. But what the heck. I'll just go for it.

"Ruby," Declan says, startling me and pulling me from my phone.

"Yeah?"

"I'm going to text you a code that you can enter on this screen." He turns my computer so I can see it. "Enter it now and then keep the code for if this happens again."

As soon as my phone pings, I open the text and type in the code.

He turns the computer toward himself again and gets back to work.

RUBY:

> Our dry humping was short-lived, but I want to do it again. And again. With fewer clothes. Maybe my feelings come from the fact that he's overly good-looking. I mean, his chest is like a rock, and I hate that I want to touch it. I hate that I told him he had to start wearing shirts. Add in his stupid cute smirk and the fact that he's smart and great with Max and just ... it's too much. It's easier to not like him. I need to be focused on myself and Max. If I did like him, instead of fixing my computer, I'd be climbing him like a pole and breaking my dry spell.

I PRESS SEND, slightly regretting that I divulged too much while venting my frustration, but they all suspected it already. It made sense to admit it. The more information they have, the better they can help me.

I let out a groan, hating how worked up I'm getting over something that will never happen.

Declan's phone pings, and I freeze.

Some might call it intuition, but I call it fear.

Fear that I just did something very, very wrong.

I grab my phone and set it in my lap, slowly turning it over to check my text messages.

Right there at the top is Declan's text thread, and right there when I open said thread is my admission to the girls.

No.

My stomach drops. My heart thuds.

No.

No.

I look up quickly. Declan hasn't touched his phone yet because he's focused on my laptop.

Okay, okay, I can work with this.

I just need a plan to steal his phone and crack the code with my super awesome tech girl skills and then delete my text. All in mere seconds.

Simple.

I could die right now.

Okay, no time to panic.

I stand.

He's still focused on the laptop.

Slowly, I walk around the back of his chair to the other side of the table. He's still focused.

He must really like computers.

I keep walking, slowly so as not to draw attention.

I casually reach out and take his phone.

Again, slowly, so nothing seems out of the—

"Why are you trying to sneak my phone?"

"Huh?" I turn and press my lips together. "Hmm."

"My phone." Declan leans back and crosses his arms as he studies me. "Why do you need it?"

"Oh, is this your phone?" I ask innocently. "I thought it was mine. My bad."

I turn to walk off, but he goes on.

"Since we have established that it's my phone, you can leave it here on the table."

Damn it.

Why would I need it?

Why?

Why, Ruby!

"I thought I'd just bring it over here and charge it for you."

I keep walking.

"Ruby, stop."

His voice is firm, in the tone he saves just for me, and I have to take a breath.

It was hot.

"Turn to face me."

That one, too.

"Why do you need my phone?"

"I …"

"The truth."

I hold my chin high.

"I … accidentally sent a text for the girls to you and I need to delete it."

His left brow lifts as he smirks.

"What does it say?"

I glare at him. "If I told you that, that would defeat the purpose of deleting it, wouldn't it?"

He shrugs. "I guess."

"So, can I have your passcode to delete it?"

"The passcode to my phone seems pretty intimate, don't you think?"

I laugh.

"If you think that's intimate, then you should read—never mind. Nope. I don't think that it is."

His gaze meets mine and turns dark.

His chest rises, and the urge to ask him what he's thinking is heavy, but I don't.

The girls, as usual, perk up, and I take a deep breath.

"Please, Declan."

He swallows and then nods.

"9292."

Relief floods me as I enter the code and all the apps on his phone appear. I tap on the text message icon, find our thread. He's watching me, but as soon as our eyes meet, he looks away and focuses on my computer again.

Just like that. He trusts me to only delete this message.

No worries or comments that I'll snoop.

No teasing about what the text could be.
I said I wanted to delete it and he was fine with it.
Fuck. Why does that make me want him even more?
I swipe on the text and delete it, then I sit down.
"Feel better?" he asks.
If only.

CHAPTER TWELVE

DECLAN

I didn't sleep much last night, and every time I woke up after dreaming of Ruby, I had to talk myself out of not un-deleting her text. I'm not proud that I know how to do these things, but right now, as I do something as mundane as drive through town, I'm still convincing myself not to do it.

But I want to know.

I need to know.

What could she have said to *the girls* that she didn't want me to know?

It has to be about the other night.

I could do it and never tell her.

But that would be considered an invasion of privacy.

Right?

Then again, the text was sent to my phone, so it's on my property, and that means I have a right to look at it.

Plus, it was about me. That's the only reason she would want to delete it, right?

I groan, get out of my truck, and head into our town's small recreation center. It's not much, but it's freshly remodeled and has a basketball court indoors where the boys and I meet far too many times a month than I'd like. Only for the sole fact that it was their idea to start playing this sport I never grew up playing, yet somehow, I have managed to be a better player than the rest of them.

I'd be fine with just hanging out at someone's house with a beer or two or even no beers, like we normally do.

I push open the front door and spot Hudson, Miles, and Luca at the front counter. The receptionist is handing them water.

"I'll take one of those," I say as I approach.

All three turn to look at me. They're smiling, but it's Luca's massive grin that stops me in my tracks.

"What?"

They each look at each other, and then Miles slugs Luca. "Bro, you're so damn obvious."

Luca slugs Miles back. "I'm not obvious. Declan has no idea what we're thinking right now."

"Oh, for fuck's sake." Hudson groans. "Now you have to tell him."

I imagine this is what it would have been like to grow up with brothers.

The teasing and arm punching. And of course, the annoying need to know what the heck Luca's talking about.

Maybe it's the fact that their sister is also keeping something from me.

These Ashers sure are something else.

I clear my throat. "Soooo."

Hudson gives in. "Luca thinks you and Ruby are going to start developing feelings for each other."

I keep my facial expression as neutral as I can.

Luca nods as if he's waiting for me to confirm that he's right. Miles looks like he'd rather be anywhere else, and Hudson has his arms crossed as he, too, waits for my response.

"Me"—I point to myself with my thumb—"and your sister."

"Yeah, I thought it was stupid, too," Miles says and heads for the court.

Is it, though? I mean, we have been living together for almost two weeks now, and the other night we almost …

"It's not stupid," Luca argues. "It's fitting."

"She's our sister," Miles goes on. "That's not Declan's style. She's like a kid to him, and as our sister she's off-limits."

Ruby is far from a kid in my eyes.

"I wouldn't say eight years makes her a kid, and are sisters off-limits?" I ask. Everyone stops to look at me.

Shit.

Why the fuck did I ask that?

"Wait for me," Linc shouts as he comes through the doors.

His steps slow as he approaches. "What's happening?"

"Declan just asked if sisters are off-limits," Hudson catches him up.

"To what?" Linc asks.

"Him," Miles answers.

Linc doesn't answer— he simply erupts into laughter. "Considering that fact mine is taken, I'd say this is a Ruby-specific question. Are you two …"

My hands go up instantly. I'm about to get bombarded with questions.

"No. No, I was thrown off by the approach to this conversation and I wanted to clarify it, but it doesn't really matter, because I can confidently say that your sister still has a strong distaste for me."

That might be a lie.

Maybe I would know if I just read her text.

"Boooo," Luca says.

Miles grunts.

Hudson just keeps watching me as if I'm going to do something to give myself away.

Which, honestly, what is there to tell? I don't even know what's going on or if anything is going on. It could have just been a weak moment that developed from the fact that we are forced to be around each other more than normal.

Convenience. Maybe that's all I was to her.

That's not what she was to me.

But, what is she to me?

"Let's just play, huh?" I suggest, moving along toward the court and letting out a breath when they all follow.

Linc jogs up to me and leans in.

"I thought Hudson had it bad with Sadie. You have three brothers to deal with."

"I'm not … there isn't anything happening."

But shit, he's right.

Dutton is already waiting for us when we get there.

"Took you guys long enough."

"Sorry," Luca speaks up first. "We were just discussing how—"

"Vegas," Hudson cuts him off. "We were talking about Vegas and how I hope you are all ready to go in two days."

Everyone seems to be fine with that answer, so we sit to change our shoes and stretch.

But of course, Luca still has more to say.

He comes up to me and speaks low enough that no one else can hear him.

"Look, I know I'm being a little extra, but I need you to know that I'd be cool with it."

"With what?"

He gives me a look that says I'm an idiot if I'm seriously asking that.

Which is fair.

"Nothing is happening," I repeat.

"Alright, but if that changes, just know you can tell me or talk to me or whatever."

I nod. "Got it."

If I talk to anyone about it, it's going to be Ruby.

"Tell me before Miles, though. He's a little more sensitive about Ruby, as you're aware. He'd never admit it, but I think it hit him the hardest when she left. They had a different connection than the rest of us growing up. He's going to be picky on the next guy she dates. It can't be anyone who could steal her from our family again."

I know some things about Ruby's background, but not all the details, so his comment stuns me more than I expect.

"And Hudson," he adds, and I find myself leaning in to hear what he's going to say. "Well, everything is different when it comes to him. He knows what it's like to lose a part of yourself and then to meet the right person who can bring you back to life."

Shit. That's deep.

"What I mean is, I think that if you can show him that you and Ruby bring out the best in each other, he'd be cool about it like me."

I chuckle.

I like knowing Ruby has her brothers looking out for her, but Luca is forgetting one big detail.

Ruby has yet to admit that we are friends. She'd never admit to us being anything more than that.

"Good to know, Luca. Thank you."

"You're welcome. Now do you have anything you want to tell me?" He grins, and it makes me laugh harder.

"Nope."

His grin falls. "Really?"

"Really. Your sister does not like me that way, or any way that I'm aware of."

He nods, his grin slowly coming back. I should get up before he says whatever he's thinking. This guy's mind goes a mile a minute.

"Okay" is all he says and stands.

Wow.

I lucked out. I think.

He turns and walks backward to where the other guys are waiting.

"But ..."

Here we go.

"You never said that *you* didn't like *her*."

Shit.

BASKETBALL WAS FILLED with weird vibes the entire time.

But I can't blame my friends.

Even though I denied it, my mind has been filled with thoughts of us.

Me and Ruby.

I thought of her through every shot I took, through driving to the store to get her a new laptop since hers will more than likely go on the fritz again, and the entire drive home.

And it was the first thing that came to mind when I walked in the door and saw her in the kitchen.

What if something more did happen between us? What if she didn't dislike me so much? How would our day to day go? Would she be more flirtatious with me?

But then the kids ran into the house, and those thoughts disappear.

I can't let my attraction for Ruby chance ruining our kids' friendship.

So the moment Ruby mentions an errand she needs to run, I offer to watch Max and Susie.

It's sort of been an unspoken agreement between us, this helping with the kids.

Speaking of Max and Susie.

It's eerily silent in here.

I glance over my shoulder to where they ran up and down the hall maybe five minutes ago.

"Susie?" I call out. It's not exactly a yell, but it's louder than normal.

No response.

I rise slowly, ready to catch the two of them doing something they shouldn't. I've learned the hard way that silence is never good. They might be older now, but that means nothing when a kid becomes curious.

"Max?" I call out this time and wait at the bottom of the steps.

Possibly three seconds go by before his head pokes out of one of the bedroom doors.

"Yeah, Dec?"

I stand taller and place my hands on my hips.

"What are you doing in your mom's room? Is Susie in there?"

It's one thing for Max to be in his mom's room, but Susie doesn't need to intrude on Ruby's space like that. Not when Ruby isn't home to make the official decision.

His head disappears and then Susie's pops out.

Just her head and neck.

They are definitely up to something in there.

"What's going on?"

"Nothing." She squeaks and her instant answer is all too telling.

"Come down here." I nod and step back so she can stand in front of me.

Susie rolls her eyes and then disappears.

"Susie, now. Max, you too."

Am I allowed to parent him?

Ruby said she'd be only a few minutes.

I think I'm good.

Both kids finally emerge, hands behind their backs. Like two deer in headlights, they stare at me.

"What are you hiding?"

"Nothing." This time the squeak is from Max.

It's when they try to slink down the hall, turning their backs away from me that I grow more serious.

"Show me. You can't go into Ruby's room and take things that are not yours."

"But I think these are supposed to be ours. One is blue and one is purple," Max defends. "Like maybe an early birthday gift."

Shit. They were snooping.

"Then you really shouldn't take it. If it's a gift, she should get to see you open it, bud."

I hold my hand out.

"Now, hand it over and go play outside like a couple of normal kids."

The kids share a look and then sigh as they both hand over the toys they stole.

Before they even touch my hand—or well, two hands because I need both to hold them—it's my turn to be a deer in headlights.

The kids run past me, shouting apologies as I stand frozen at the bottom of the stairs, staring at the kitchen in front of me and trying not to glance down at the not one but two vibrators in my hands.

Two.

She has two vibrators.

Ruby Asher.

And they are in my hands.

What the fuck kind of toys did those kids think these were?

I've failed somewhere.

What the fuck?

Ruby's going to kill me.

Against my better judgment, I glance down at the purple one. It has ribbed edges.

I'll be honest. This is my first time holding a dildo, and I jumped right in with two.

Am I obsessing over the fact that there are two? Yes, yes, I fucking am. Ruby Asher isn't as innocent as I thought she was.

And I'm not supposed to think of her this way.

Ever.

Fuck.

These days I can't seem to stop.

I hold the purple one up; clearly, a little bravery has appeared.

I observe each side of it.

It must be a manual one, as I don't see any buttons.

And how big is this thing? How far does she ... no, no, I cannot think like this about her.

The other night was bad enough. I'll never get the image of her on my lap or the softness of her skin under my fingers out of my head.

I can't be thinking of her like this now.

She's helping me by letting us live with her, and I'd have to deal with not one, not two, but three of her brothers as it was made perfectly clear at the gym today. And the kids. The kids are our priority. How would it affect them if this didn't work out?

I let the hand with the purple vibrator drop as I glance at the other one.

Fun.

The blue one plays with her clit, too.

The image of Ruby lying on her bed using both of these at the same time stirs my cock to life. I can see her using the purple one, while the other vibrates against her—

"What are you doing?"

I spin, the blue dildo dropping from my hand.

Both of our gazes fall to the floor where it landed between us.

"Oh my God." Nothing about her gasp helps the situation in my pants.

She picks it up and then spots the purple one in my hand.

She hits me with a glare that could murder me in my sleep.

Shit.

I hold my hands up. "This isn't what it looks like."

I slowly step toward her, holding out the purple dildo to her.

She takes it from me on a growl and is about to walk past me when Luca walks into the house.

"Declan, just the man I was looking for."

It all happens in a blur.

I jump.

Ruby jumps.

Then Ruby tosses the dildos on the couch.

I move quickly to sit on them so her brother doesn't see them and put together the fact that his sister and I were just standing in the middle of the house with two vibrators.

No way in hell am I letting that happen after the conversations this morning.

So yep. That's me. Declan Young. A man who not only has

officially held two dildos in his hand today but is now sitting on them.

I glance at Ruby, whose eyes are wide, and her mouth is dropped open. Slowly, it turns into a grin.

"Why did you need Declan?" she asks cooly, as if what just happened was normal.

"I want to take the kids to The Marina for the afternoon and then for dinner. Are you two cool with that?"

"Doesn't that mean you need me too?" Ruby asks.

Luca shrugs. "I knew you'd say yes, so really I just need Declan to say yes for Susie."

Both Asher siblings look at me.

Can they see that I'm sweating?

"Sounds great," I answer quickly. "Have fun."

The sooner he's gone, the sooner I can stand up.

"Sweet. Bye!"

Luca walks out the door, passing Max.

"I forgot to give Declan this." Her son holds up a tiny remote. He presses a button with his thumb, and instantly my ass begins to tingle.

Ruby erupts into laughter and takes the remote but doesn't turn it off.

I know she can hear it.

This thing is fucking intense.

And she puts it inside her.

Fuck.

That's hot.

Now I'm even harder than before.

I'm a grown man. Why do I have no control right now?

I need a shower.

I also need the people in this room to vanish so I can walk out with a bit of dignity.

She hugs Max goodbye while my kid yells goodbye through

the door and then the door closes and I spring up like my life depends on it.

"So, the kids took them and gave them to you." Ruby chuckles. She reaches for her toys, but I beat her to it.

I hold up the one still vibrating.

"Is this one your favorite?"

Her smile drops, and her gaze turns heated.

She takes a deep breath, and just when I think she's going to have some smart-ass remark for me asking such a personal question, she simply nods.

"How often do you use it?"

I step closer, letting my curiosity lead the way.

She swallows.

"I …"

Then her cheeks turn the sexiest shade of pink as she looks away, clicking the remote off.

"I …"

"You can tell me, Ruby. It'll be our little secret."

Her gaze flicks back to mine.

"Our little secret can be the fact that I even own these. No one knows. Which is how it should be."

I nod.

"So, you've never used these with anyone?"

She shakes her head. "Why are you so curious?"

I don't know how to answer her, so I remain quiet.

It's her turn to step closer.

"Does the idea of them and me turn you on?"

I smirk.

Her slight hand reaches forward, taking the vibrators from me.

"You don't have to answer me." She looks down. "Your gray sweatpants are giving you away."

Shit.

"To be fair, while you'll be downstairs thinking of me and my toys, I'll be thinking of you in these sweatpants."

This isn't us. This isn't how we act.

"Fair's fair, right?" I ask.

"Sure. Anything else you want to know before I put these back?"

The words fall from my mouth before I can think better of it.

"Do you use them at the same time?"

A slow smile forms on her lips.

The same lips that have me captivated and wishing that I would have stolen a taste of them the other night.

She takes a step backward. She isn't going to answer me.

Then she turns and starts to jog up the stairs.

"Wait!" I call out when she gets to the top step. "I got you something."

Now is as good a time as any to change the subject before I do something one of us might regret later.

"Okay," she laughs. "Let me just put these away first."

She hurries to her room as I grab the computer from my truck. She's just reaching the bottom of the stairs when I step in the door.

Her eyes drop instantly to the box.

"What's that?"

"I got you a new computer. While I recovered files yesterday, I have a feeling it'll happen again. This way you're all—"

"I don't want it." She crosses her arms and steps back.

"You need a new computer, Ruby."

"Then I'll buy one myself. I ... I don't have anything to offer you in return, and right now I can't—"

"It's a gift. I don't need or want anything in return."

"Everything comes at a price, Declan. I can't take it."

"This,"—I hold the box up—"does not come with strings. It comes with *you being a gifted graphic designer who built her own company*, which is pretty badass by the way, *who needs a computer that works*. I know computers, and this one is perfect for what you want to achieve."

She just looks at the box and then at me again. I can see in the way her mouth twists and the way her fingers drill against her arms that she's thinking it over.

"No strings?" she asks softly.

"Not a single one."

She nods slowly and then steps toward me.

"Can you help me set it up and back up my current files?"

I beam.

"I'd love to."

We spend the next hour getting everything set to go so she can get to work. It's a great distraction from the afternoon's events.

I grab a bottle of water and head for the stairs, leaving Ruby to work alone at the table.

"Declan?" she says. I stop on the top step.

"Yeah?"

"Two vibrators." She lifts her head and winks at me. "That's the only way to use them."

Fuck.

I jog down the steps to the basement to put as much distance between us as possible.

Then impulse gets the best of me and I'm coding my phone to show me the deleted message.

RUBY:

> Our dry humping was short-lived, but I want to do it again. And again. With fewer clothes. Maybe my feelings come from the fact that he's overly good-looking. I mean, his chest is like a rock, and I hate that I want to touch it. I hate that I told him he had to start wearing shirts. Add in his stupid cute smirk and the fact that he's smart and great with Max and just … it's too much. It's easier to not like him. I need to be focused on myself and Max. If I did like him, instead of fixing my computer, I'd be climbing him like a pole and breaking my dry spell.

I DROP to my bed and blow out a breath.

It's not overly bad, but it's not good either.

Because despite the relationship we have, if Ruby ever tried to climb me like a pole, I don't think I could stop her.

I wouldn't want to.

CHAPTER THIRTEEN

RUBY

When I was a kid, I blurted out anything that came to mind. As the baby girl of the family, I could get away with anything.

There was never any punishment.

But yesterday, the vibrator incident with Declan, I wish someone had told me to quit talking.

Especially when I said that I'd be thinking of him in his sweatpants.

Of course I would be.

Look at the man.

I'm not blind, but I'm clearly horny. First, I dry hump him in the living room, and then I'm telling him I use both vibrators at once.

God. I even had time to calm down from the discussion and still came back to it.

I swear. Me. Declan. Alone. Brain malfunction.

Not to mention, I don't actually use them at the same time. Just the idea of that confuses me.

Fuck.

Why would I even say that?

I groan, glancing at the clock.

Five A.M.

I guarantee that no one else is awake right now.

With our flights leaving tomorrow morning for Vegas, I won't have any alone time for a while.

My eyes move to the top drawer of my nightstand.

No one would know.

I reach in and grab the one he assumed is my favorite.

I close my eyes and slip my hands under the covers.

My sleep shorts are loose enough that I can leave them on, and the fact that I don't wear underwear to bed is convenient right now.

A vision of Declan and I in the living room takes over. The memory of how hard he felt underneath me feels as if it were happening again right now.

I press the tip of the vibrator to my core, and it slips inside. I didn't need to add gel. No, just thoughts of the man living downstairs has me wet enough to do this right now.

My back bows a little as I slide it farther and a new image pops into my head: he and I standing in the kitchen with the vibrators in my hand.

I imagine him stepping closer to me until the back of my legs hit the table. He'd pick me up, strip my pants off, then spread my legs to eat me right there because he has no self-control, and I'd let him because I don't either.

And since no one has ever done that to me, I want to know what it feels like.

He'd flick his tongue over me, over and over, dirty words coming from his mouth between each one, just the way I read them in books.

You're so wet.

This is all for me.

I can't wait to be inside of you.

This pussy is perfect.

Then I'd beg him to just put it in and fuck me.

I don't need sweet foreplay to drag this out. I need to get off.

I slide the vibrator as far as it can go, the smaller end touching my clit. Then I turn it on, and my entire body starts to shake with the vibrations.

I come quickly with Declan on my mind, and I let myself ride it out until the tingle that courses through my veins fades.

I slide the vibrator out and begin to catch my breath.

Oh, God.

What did I just do?

———

I'VE NEVER BEEN SO thankful for being busy before. Cleaning, laundry, and packing have been more enjoyable than ever before.

"Your dad will be here soon, so let's make sure your bag is packed and ready," I say to Max when he steps inside from the backyard where he was playing soccer with Susie.

"Yes! I can't wait to see him." He runs to his room.

As if he knew we were talking about him, a horn honks out front. Colt.

"He's here, Max!" I shout just as Declan appears at the top of the stairs.

His eyes meet mine, and I look away instantly.

Guilt from this morning hits me hard, but my heart pounds harder.

I've been avoiding him all day because of it.

Like, I have this need to tell him so that I can be free of it, but I know that will never happen because I'd be mortified.

I move to rush out of the kitchen to greet Colt just as Declan steps into it. I turn to shuffle sideways, but my body still brushes against his.

His hand lingers, his fingers grazing my stomach as we pass each other.

I freeze, my skin hot under his touch.

His head is down, and his eyes are closed.

Relief floods me. I don't know what would happen if his gaze locked onto mine. Would he read my mind? Would I blurt out something embarrassing?

The sound of a car door slamming pulls me from the moment.

I dash out the front door and don't look back.

"You made it!" I say, meeting Colt halfway down the driveway and wrapping him in a hug.

He hugs me back.

"I've been here many times, Ruby. I'm not going to get lost."

I swat his shoulder and step back.

Colt's eyes are on the front porch.

Declan.

"Look, I know we talked about this, but is everything going okay? Do you still think it's a good move? You weren't too sure about it before."

I tilt my head as if to say *are you being serious*? and then I sigh, preparing myself to do something I don't do often but am mature enough to know it's the right move.

"He's a good guy, Colt. He's great with the kids, and Max looks up to him. It's actually been nice having him here."

Colt's eyes flick to me, and then he grins. "Do you like him?"

"What? No."

I roll my eyes to drive the point home. "It's actually a little annoying, how nice he is. I mean, just watching him with his daughter is so freaking cute, it makes me want to puke sometimes."

"Come on, Ruby." He nudges me with his elbow. "Just because it didn't work between us doesn't mean I don't know you. We lived together for seven years, remember? This man gets a reaction out of you that I was never able to get. His choices leave him on your mind most of the day, don't they?"

I know he isn't saying this to make me feel guilty, but I think a part of me always will. Colt tried to make it work with us. More so than me. I accepted that we weren't a match long before he could. Image is important to his family, so their teenage son getting a woman pregnant and then she up and moved to some small town in Wyoming probably makes his mother cringe. I have no doubt that my moving is why his father feels the need to check in on me with payment updates. To be sure I didn't leave thinking my debt would be waived, I'm sure.

I don't know what Colt said to them after I left, but he and I decided together that raising Max here was best, that's all that matters to me.

Sometimes, I think Colt wishes he lived a different life than the one dealt to him, so when the opportunity for me and Max to leave arose, he didn't want us to miss it.

"Ruby?" Colt says softly and tilts his head to look at me. "All good?"

I nod.

"Yes, sorry. Just a little lost in thought."

"I see that and I—"

Before he can get another word out, the front door opens, and Max and Susie run out in a flash.

Declan continues to stand on the porch, his gaze sweeping over Colt and me.

My entire body becomes alert, and as much as I hate to admit it, my nipples harden from the look Declan is giving me.

His gaze turns dark as he crosses his arms, still never breaking eye contact with me.

"Well," Colt whispers with a teasing tone, "whatever you *don't* feel, seems like he *doesn't* feel it either."

I don't have time to reply before Max practically launches himself into Colt's arms.

"Dad! You made it!"

"I missed you so much," Colt says and then sets him down to ruffle his hair.

"Same. This is Susie," Max says with the biggest grin on his face. "My best friend. She's super cool."

"Hi." Susie waves and then shyly spins to run back to her dad.

"And that's Declan. He told me not to call him Mr. Young."

"That's great. I better go meet him."

Max grabs his dad's hand and pulls him toward the front porch. I follow behind them, listening to the two of them chat. It's hard not to.

"You're going to like him. He's extra smart. He's into tech stuff, just like you."

"That's pretty neat."

"Yeah, Mom's computer crashed, and he fixed it, and then he bought her a new one."

I don't need to look up to feel Colt staring at me.

We hit the steps and Max starts to introduce them right away.

"Dad, this is Declan. Declan, this is my dad."

My heart swells at how happy Max looks right now.

Colt and Declan shake hands.

"It's nice to meet you," Colt says.

"Likewise. Max talks about you a lot."

"He's mentioned you a couple of times, but I have to admit, I think I might know more about Susie at this point."

Me, Declan, and Colt all laugh, and my gaze finds Declan's again. It's like my insides turn to mush.

I turn for the door to avoid anyone being able to read my facial expression.

"Let's go in; it's hot. Max's things are ready to go."

"Where is Susie headed for the weekend?" Colt asks as we step inside.

Declan closes the door and comes to stand by me.

I sidestep to give us some distance.

Declan widens his stance and crosses his arms.

"My parents are driving up from Wind Valley. They should be here any moment."

"Are they staying here?"

Declan nods.

"Then why are Max and I leaving?" Colt shifts his gaze to mine. "Why don't I get a room at the lodge and stay here for the weekend? Max can still stay with me, but during the day, we can be here or by the water so the kids can play. We both know that would be a more enjoyable weekend for him."

I smirk at Colt.

"What are you trying to get out of?"

"Nothing."

His quick answer isn't convincing.

"Honestly," I start. "Max would love that, but it's your call. They both already know they won't spend the weekend together."

"Do you think your parents would mind?" Colt asks Declan.

He doesn't reply right away. Instead, he's watching Colt, clearly thinking over his answer.

Finally, he says, "I think they would like that."

Then he clears his throat, "Excuse me."

He moves for the stairs and jogs down.

"Do you think I offended him?" Colt asks.

I shrug. "No. He would tell you. I don't know what just happened. Do you want to stay for dinner?" I ask and then wave him toward the kitchen.

"Yeah, just let me step outside to call the lodge."

Once he's outside, I glance back at the stairs. My feet move toward it as if it's the most natural thing in the world.

Something just happened that upset Declan, and I want to know what it was.

I need to know.

I take one step down and pause.

We don't exactly have that type of relationship, though. So the chances of him telling me what's on his mind are slim.

Still, I've never seen him like that.

I take another step, ready to push past our history and see how I can help him, but both kids come running up the steps.

"Am I really staying here?" Max asks and his eyes light up.

"We sure are," Colt says, walking back into the house. "As soon as Susie's grandparents are here, let's make a plan."

"Yes!" Both kids cheer and then rush to Colt, talking a mile a minute.

I glance back down the stairs, waiting for Declan to follow, but he doesn't.

I take it as a clear sign that he wants to be alone right now.

But as I cook dinner and set the table, my mind is only on one thing.

Declan.

———

DECLAN IS a different person by the time he returns upstairs for dinner.

His parents got a late start to their drive, so they aren't here yet. Like Colt, they are staying at the lodge for the weekend.

Part of me thought I'd meet his parents, but now I don't think I will. I'm not so sure I'm up for meeting the parents of another wealthy son.

"So, wait," Colt says and holds his hand up. Dinner is long over, and the kids are inside playing games while Declan, Colt, and I sit out back with a drink. "You're *the* Declan Young. As in Young Technologies Software?" Colt leans forward in his chair. "The CEO."

Declan nods and part of me is proud that Colt is impressed, which feels unfamiliar. It shouldn't matter for so many reasons.

"Guilty," Declan answers.

"You do know who I am, right?"

"Colt," I scold.

"I don't mean it in a *look how rich I am* way, Ruby. I mean it as in, is it not insane that the man you're living with is the owner of my dad's biggest rival company? I mean, if you thought my dad didn't care for you, you should hear him talk about Declan. He *hates* him. Sorry about him, by the way. The way he does business is wild to me."

I ignore the part about his dad not caring for me and go to the next part.

"Rivals? Really? Did you know who Max's dad was before you moved in?" I cast my question to Declan.

I knew both were part of the tech world, but that could mean anything. I didn't realize they were so similar.

"I was aware, but I didn't think it affected anything, so I never brought it up."

"It doesn't, but is that weird?" This time my question is directed to Colt.

"Yeah, but not in a bad way. Declan, or his assistant anyway, deals with my dad directly and not me, which is probably why I never put two and two together. I wonder if my dad has though."

I grunt.

Oh, I'm sure he has.

"Are there rules against this?" I ask, and both of them laugh.

"No," Colt says. "There are no rules on this."

"I wouldn't even know how to draft that." Declan chuckles. "Owner agrees to never become roommates with the mother and son of the competing company."

They both laugh again, but this isn't funny.

"I don't think I'm into this."

"What?" Colt asks.

"You two getting along."

They are alike in a lot of ways, but also not.

I don't know how to feel about that.

"Why not? Declan seems fun."

"I tell her that all the time, and she still argues with me."

Declan tips the top of his beer toward me before taking a sip.

My gaze sweeps over his tattoos. "You've never once said you're fun," I point out and cross my arms.

His head volleys. "Probably because I'm too busy trying to figure out why you don't like me."

"Sorry," I say on a shrug.

"Wait," Colt cuts in. "You never told him?"

"No," I snap and then hold a finger in front of my lips to silence my son's father.

"You know why?" Declan sits up. "Tell me."

"No," I answer for him.

"Ruby, come on. Help the guy out."

"Yeah, Ruby, help a guy out," Declan repeats.

"Okay." I smile and stand. "It's time for Colt to go and for us to finish packing."

"Fine, fine. Don't tell me," Declan says, standing as well and walking behind me to the sliding door.

At least he listens.

"Just keep not liking me. I mean, it *is* easier that way."

I spin to face him.

"What did you just say?"

His eyes go wide, and he takes a step back.

"Umm, that you not liking me comes easy to you."

I step toward him and again he steps back.

I never break eye contact.

His eyes dart to the left; his throat bobs on a swallow,

I gasp.

"Declan, tell me you didn't do what I think you did."

"I did not."

"Oh my god!" My arms flail. "You answered that so fast, I know you did it."

"What did he do?" Colt asks with a grin.

"He undeleted a text I sent him and then read it."

"Why was it deleted?" Colt asks and his grin only gets bigger.

"It doesn't matter."

"I had to know. Especially after the other night," Declan says.

"What happened the other night?"

"Nothing," Declan and I answer at the same time.

Colt gives us a double thumbs-up. "I'll just go say good night to Max and Susie."

He disappears into the house, and I fold my arms and glare at Declan.

I don't even know what to say. I'm so, so, so …

"I'm sorry," he blurts out before I can put words together. "I knew it was wrong the moment I did it."

I know he's waiting for me to say something, but I still don't know what to say. Saying I feel violated feels wrong after what I did this morning.

The longer he stares at me, the more my eyes sting, and when I know I'm about to cry, I turn for the door.

"Ruby, wait." He grabs my hand and pulls me back. Only he tugs more than enough to pull me back and spin me into him. He wraps the hand not holding mine around my waist to stop my momentum.

On instinct, I look up into his eyes.

"I really am sorry."

The sincerity in his voice is like a warm blanket wrapping me up.

He really means it.

"Thank you," I manage to whisper.

He doesn't let go of me, and I don't let go of him.

His gaze shifts to my lips, and I inhale, closing my eyes.

All too quickly, I feel his hand leave mine, and my body goes cold in the distance he gives us.

He clears his throat. "I'll uh, let you go say goodbye to Colt."

I turn quickly and rush inside.

He was going to kiss me and chose not to.

I was going to let him, and he turned me down.

I step into the living room and spot the kids each in their own spot, now watching a movie.

"Where did your dad go?" I ask Max.

"He left. Said he would text you."

I hear the sliding door open and close, but I don't turn to look.

I can't look at him right now.

Not when I don't know what just happened—or rather what didn't just happen.

My phone pings right then.

I pull it from my back pocket and stare at the text.

COLT:

Please tell me he kissed you. Also, full support
here with anything you choose, but please
keep Max in mind if you start something. I
know you will, but yeah. Dinner was great.
Night!

I EXIT the thread and groan.

Is this really my life right now?

CHAPTER FOURTEEN

DECLAN

I pull my headphones out of my ears as we reach Wind Valley. The car ride to the airport went quickly for me because I was on my tablet the entire time, working on his deal, but it probably went the quickest for Linc. He got stuck with the middle seat in the back between me and Miles and still managed to sleep the entire drive. How? I have no clue. Even with headphones in, I know Luca talked the entire time about all the things we could do in Vegas, while Hudson reminded him that this weekend is about the bride and groom, and Miles was on the phone with Quinn for most of it.

They were either talking or texting, which seems a bit excessive considering the girls were in the car behind us for the entire drive.

But I'll give him the benefit of the doubt—Quinn just got back to Lovers yesterday after being away on her latest trip.

He missed her.

I get it.

Hudson steers his truck through the airport parking lot

looking for an open spot, probably with two next to each other since the girls are in Sadie's 4Runner.

I slip my phone from my pocket and look at the last text from my mom.

It's a picture of Colt playing in the sand with Susie and Max. They seem to be covering him with sand so that only his head shows.

Susie is having fun.

But my heart breaks a little for her at the same time.

She'll never know what it's like to have two parents who put her first. Colt jumped at the idea of staying in Lovers just so Max and Susie, a little girl he'd met for all of two seconds, could spend it together. He knew his son would have more fun with her than just with him and so he chose that route for the next three days.

He chose his son's happiness.

He chose my daughter's happiness.

And fuck, I'm getting all choked up again thinking about it.

The same way I did when he suggested it yesterday.

Not to mention the relationship Ruby has with Colt. They are friends. Actual friends. Not just for show to their families and friends. Real fucking friends.

I'm jealous as heck about it.

It was a bonus that Colter Davenport is nothing like his father. I wanted to ask him more about his father's intentions with Collins Corp last night, but Colt hasn't been included in anything, so I don't know how much he actually knows.

Still, I wish it were him that I was dealing with and not his father.

"Get out of the truck, now," Hudson says to Luca and then points at Miles. "And hang up. She's right there."

That older brother's annoyed tone makes me grin and earns a chuckle.

This trip is exactly what I need right now.

I need to relax and let loose, take a break from work, and forget about the things I can't change.

Not only with my kid, but also how I had Ruby in my arms last night and everything inside of me screamed to kiss her, but then my mind re-reads her text. Despite being attracted to me, she doesn't want this, so I backed off out of respect and hated every minute of it.

Yeah, Vegas sounds like a great plan.

Maybe the guys will branch off at some point and I'll find someone to take my mind off Ruby.

I groan.

Who am I kidding?

I'd probably think of her the whole time.

We all pile out of the truck, grab our bags from the bed, and wait for the girls to do the same.

Miles and Quinn start making out as if it's been a lifetime since they saw each other.

Luca kisses Shay's forehead.

Hudson slings his arms around Sadie's shoulders, leaning in for a temple kiss, and then he grabs her bag.

Linc stands next to Brooke, who is texting on her phone.

Then there is Ruby, who is looking around the group the same way I am. Her eyes meet mine, and she forces a smile.

"Where are Dutton and Grace?" she asks.

"Here!" Grace rushes up. "Dutton drives like a grandma, so I made him pull over and switch so I could drive."

"I don't drive like a grandma," he defends himself and then slugs his sister. She takes a fight stance, and Dutton steps back, glaring at her.

"Alright." Luca claps loudly, gaining the attention of the group. "Are we all ready?"

Miles laughs. "The fact that we are standing here should be an obvious yes."

"I don't see Grace's bag," Luca says.

"Oh shit." Grace runs to her car and comes back, bag rolling next to her.

Luca looks at his brother like *told you so*. This is going to either be a long-ass trip or one I'll remember for a long time. My bets are on the latter.

"Let's go," Luca says and waves for all of us to follow behind him and Shay.

Two by two, the group heads into the airport, leaving the tail end for me and Ruby.

She glances at me, and just when I'm about to smile, she rolls her eyes and walks off.

I sigh and follow.

I don't even have to wonder why I got that one.

Nope, now I'm just left wondering why she's mad that I didn't kiss her.

That's what she wanted, wasn't it?

———

I SHOULD HAVE KNOWN that the seats would also be paired up. When Hudson asked everyone for their information to book, I thought that the guys and girls would sit separately.

I take my seat, waiting for some of the others in our party to board along with a few other passengers. Wind Valley Airport isn't large by any means, which means the planes that fly out aren't very big either. Our group has twelve people—that's about half the plane.

I watch as the guys each take their seats with their girls. Then Brooke with Grace and Linc with Dutton.

I let out a sigh as soon as I feel her standing next to me.

"I know you have long legs and whatnot, but if I sit by the window, there is a high chance that I'll puke."

I glance up at Ruby, my head jerking back.

"Seriously?"

She nods. "Trust me, I'm not excited about it either."

I stare at her for a moment, searching for any sign of her messing with me, but she shrugs. I unbuckle my seat belt and slide over.

The plane has two seats on each side of the aircraft, so by the time she sits, we are rubbing arms.

I adjust my legs, with one leg taking up a bit of her space.

She twists to make room but doesn't say a word.

I don't know whether her silence is because she's waiting for me to say something, or if it's because I'm starting to get the feeling she isn't a fan of flying. But I do know I'm disappointed that she isn't attempting even a little conversation.

"How many flights do you think you've been on in your life?" I ask.

"More than fifty."

I let out a whistle. "That was a fast answer."

"Well, Max is eight, and he and I have flown home three times a year since he was born. I also took a couple of flights before he was born."

I nod slowly.

"So, he's an expert flier?"

"Who loves the window seat." She forces a smile. Then her eyes flash to the window, and she looks away quickly.

"We haven't even started moving."

"I know."

"Just looking at it makes you sick?"

"Just thinking about it makes me sick."

So flying isn't her thing.

Got it.

I close the window shade.

"Susie isn't a fan of flying either. The take-offs and landings always put her on edge," I tell her.

"You're just saying that to make me feel better."

"I'm not. It's true."

And distraction always worked best with her.

"So did Max get to see you freak out a little like this or did you keep it together?"

She lets out a soft laugh.

"Oh, I have to keep it together. I don't want to freak him out too."

"Well, Ruby Asher, lucky for you, you don't have to pretend on this flight for my sake. Freak all you want. I'll be right here."

Her head remains resting against the headrest, but she rolls it to look at me with a smile.

I can't help but smile back.

Maybe she won't be mad at me for the entire trip.

"I hope you still say that if I throw up all over you."

I let out a chuckle and nod.

"Guess we'll find out."

The flight attendant's voice comes over the speaker, informing us that everyone is on the plane and that we will be moving soon.

Just as the words leave her mouth, the plane jerks to back up and Ruby's hand slaps down on mine resting on the armrest that we share.

Her fingers immediately curl around my hand.

I don't know if it's because I'm aware that she needs some type of comfort and distraction at the moment or because I believe something between us changed recently, but I roll my hand under hers and let her fingers lace with mine.

She doesn't jerk, she just squeezes tighter as we start moving.

Everyone else on the plane is going about their day, chatting, reading, or watching a movie, but not Ruby. No, Ruby is sitting here with her eyes squeezed closed so she can't see a single thing happening around her. She's probably chanting something in her head on repeat to distract herself from listening to the stewardess.

Her hand in mine grips tighter, so I reach up and turn her fan on, adjusting it until I see the hair around her face blow slightly.

She lets out a breath but still doesn't open her eyes.

I take this moment to admire her.

Typically, we don't sit this close, so having a moment to take in her high rosy cheekbones and the few freckles scattered over her small nose is nice. Heck, this is the first time I've noticed that she has three piercings in each ear.

These little details are 100 percent all her.

I always knew Ruby was pretty.

But these last couple of weeks with her have made me see her in a new light. One I'm starting to like just a little too much.

And one I have no idea what to do about.

CHAPTER FIFTEEN

RUBY

Slot machines, music, and stale air surround us as we step into the MGM. We form a line at the check-in desk, with Hudson and Sadie in front. In fact, it's a line of couples until you get to the end, where it is me and Declan pulling up the rear.

Just like at the airport and just like when I was seated by him on the plane.

I glance over my shoulder to see him following, but he's looking at his phone. It is as if the noise of the casino didn't faze him at all. Me, however? Although excited to be in a different world for the weekend, my overstimulated anxiety kicked in the moment our Uber turned onto the Strip.

"I'll go check us in since I put all the rooms under my name to get a block together," Luca says. Shay's hand is basically glued to his as the next open receptionist waves them over.

"What should we do first?" Brooke asks, gazing around the room. Her eyes settle on one of the roulette tables closest to us.

"Gamble and have a couple of drinks?" Grace offers.

"Okay." Brooke nods. "But I gave myself a gambling limit, so if I blow it all in the first five minutes, I need a backup plan."

"Don't blow it all then," Dutton says.

Brooke flashes him a glare but doesn't respond. She turns and starts talking quietly to Grace.

I try not to smirk at how the two of them sound awfully similar to Declan and me, except I'm not so sure that's Declan and me anymore. Sharing a roof these past couple of weeks has shown me a different side of him.

And then there was the couch moment.

And last night.

And he bought me a new computer out of pure kindness.

And he was pretty sweet on the plane.

And as much as I hate to admit this, Declan Young might actually be friend material.

Except the things we have done and the things going through my mind aren't things you do with your friends.

"So, there is a slight hiccup," Luca says. "We are short one room."

It's clear that his comment is directed at me.

"How?" I ask "And why are you looking at me?"

"Because he suggested that you and Declan share a room," Shay answers for him.

"What? No," I say with a little too much squeak, drawing attention from the group.

"What's wrong?" Declan asks. He clearly didn't hear my brother.

"Nothing. Just my brother losing his mind."

Luca ignores me. "The other option is that one of you gets a room to yourself while the other tags on as a third in another room or stays at another hotel."

"Who are we talking about?" Declan asks.

"Us, and no." I cross my arms. "We can get another room."

Luca scrunches his nose. "They are booked."

"Doubtful," I say and move to march around him, but Shay stops me.

"Do hotels here really run out of available rooms?" Grace asks.

"Yes," Luca answers. "They have suites open, but it's only two nights, Ruby. The cost isn't worth it."

I sigh. "Who is rooming with who?"

"Me and Shay, Miles and Quinn, Hudson and Sadie, Dutton and Linc, Grace and Brooke, and then Carver and Archer from Hudson's old team are here later. That leaves the last room for you and Declan."

"Linc," I pull out my motherly sweetness for him since he's already talking to a waitress to get a drink, "Can Declan room with you and Dutton?"

"That's about one too many dicks for me in a small room, Ruby," Dutton cuts in.

"Is that honestly the only way you could have answered that?" Brooke snaps.

Dutton ignores her.

I smirk. They're cute.

"I could room with Brooke and Grace, right?" I glance at my girls.

Grace smiles. "Of course, but keep in mind that's three girls to one bathroom, and it can get crowded fast. But I'm good with that if you two are."

Brooke nods, but Grace is right. Getting ready would take twice as long. I could sleep in their room and then get ready in Declan's. I'd have to haul my things back and forth, which is fine. Or at least keep my toothbrush in my purse so I don't forget it.

I let out a breath and look at Declan.

"I'll splurge for a suite so you can have the room," he says, moving toward the reception desk.

Of course he would. Of course he would jump to be the one to make me feel comfortable right now.

I let him take about two steps.

Luca intended for the block of rooms to be together, and if Declan gets a different one, that will defeat that purpose. And what if he does get a suite alone and then it's weird between us because I couldn't find it in me to be kind and share a room, and we go back to how things were before he moved in?

Do I want that?

"Wait. I mean, we already live together, right? The least complicated answer would be to just ... suck it up and not be upset over this."

He chuckles. "You're the only one who is upset about this, Ruby."

"You're not?"

"It's like you said, we already live together. What could you possibly do in this place to surprise me that you don't do at home?"

After the text I accidentally sent him, the living room, and then the vibrator incident ... there are a lot of things I could do to surprise him here, but it's silly to even think about that kind of connection with Declan. He's barely my friend and what? I just want to skip all that to jump his bones?

All because I'm in Vegas.

With no kid.

And about to be sharing a room with him.

Don't forget he had the opportunity to kiss you and didn't take it.

I nod slowly. "Right. Then it should be no problem at all."

"Great! Because I already told the receptionist yes, and here are your keys," Luca says and sticks both his hands out.

"If you already told them, why even ask?"

He shrugs.

"I figured that one of you was going to be in that room either way. It just makes sense to share it."

I roll my eyes as he and Shay turn away.

"Wait, aren't you going to give him a speech on don't touch my sister and treat her kindly or whatever?"

Hudson, who must have been listening, breaks into a fit of laughter, followed by Luca and Declan.

"I think that's the last thing we need to worry about," Hudson says, sharing a look with Declan that I don't care for before he then claps his hands together. "Let's all go get settled and then meet down here in an hour. We have an early dinner and the first show. Possibly a club and drinks after if we are all up for it."

"Oh, I'm still up for it," Sadie says.

She'd mentioned at girls' night once that a club was her one request.

Hudson slips his arms around Sadie's shoulder and leads her toward the elevators. Quinn is laughing at something Miles said as he whispers in her ear as they follow. I have no idea where Brooke or Grace went, nor do I see Dutton and Linc now.

I sigh, following behind Declan, who still seems to be completely unfazed by all this.

Which is the normal way to go about it, obviously. I'm just overthinking.

Sharing a room for two nights is going to be no big deal. It's not like we have to share a bed or anything. I can change in the bathroom since it has a door, and my things will stay on my side of the room.

All is going to be fine, and this weekend is going to be great.

The elevator doors open, and the eight of us try to pile in, but with a rolling suitcase per person, Declan and I don't make the cut.

"Sorry, see you soon!" Sadie says just as the doors close.

I'm too stunned to speak.

This might be my overthinking brain again, but it sure feels like this trip has been filled with moment after moment of Declan and I unexpectedly ending up alone together.

"Everything okay?" he asks.

"Everything is fine."

"When was the last time you took a trip without Max?"

I let out a laugh. "Never. I've had my weekends here or there when Colt wanted him or when I needed to get things done, but for an actual vacation, nope. Never."

"Well, that's the problem then. You just need to remember how to relax."

The doors open on our floor and I head for our room.

I refrain from a comeback because the truth of the matter is, I do have a problem.

It's just not what he thinks it is.

And, at this moment, my brain can think of only one way to relax.

Despite what I'm saying, I can't remember the last time I was as excited as I am right now to be sharing a room with Declan.

CHAPTER SIXTEEN

DECLAN

When I was in college, I had friends who would talk about their big adventures in Vegas. If that's what you want to call them. They would tell me about the girls they met and fooled around with and how they drank until their debit cards were declined and how they passed out by the pool and got a killer sunburn. The time of their lives, they called it.

Sounds like a total nightmare to me.

Those stories were on my mind until the moment it was decided that Ruby and I would share a room.

It wasn't like I expected this trip to turn out the way it did for those college friends, but still, the idea of letting loose and getting a smidge rowdy had occurred to me.

Now, I'm sharing a room with the woman who has done nothing but occupy every single bit of the free time my mind has. And then some. I'm thinking about her even when I shouldn't be.

Ruby steps out of the elevator first. The rest of the group is nowhere in sight, so it seems they've already disappeared into their rooms.

She pauses for a split moment to read the sign with the room numbers and then she heads down the hall, leading the way to what is about to be one of my top three challenging weekends. Right behind the first weekend we had Susie and the first weekend Susie's mom left us. In all three, I've had no fucking clue what I'm doing.

I'm attracted to Ruby. To her body and her mind and, if I'm not careful, this weekend very well might be the weekend where she finds out just how much.

Not that her sitting in my lap hinted at it or anything.

Or when I almost kissed her.

Shit.

She might already know and is choosing not to acknowledge it.

Without a word, she stops and holds the key card to the door. The green light shines, and she pushes the door open.

Still, I follow behind her, letting her take the lead on the vibe she wants in this situation.

Again, she stops suddenly and I almost bump into her.

"I'm going to kill my brother," she groans and then walks further into the room, letting go of her suitcase when she's next to the couch.

Like most rooms, the bathroom is to our right, and just past that is a little kitchen area with a two-person table. The mini living room is next to that, with the TV in the corner and the bed across from the couch.

The bed.

One.

And by the looks of it, it's barely made for two people.

Ruby sits on the corner of it and closes her eyes.

She clearly doesn't want to be in this situation, despite her saying she was fine, and I can fix this.

I back up toward the door.

"I'll get another room."

"What?" her gaze snaps to mine. "Why?"

"Because,"—I hold out my hand and gesture to the room—"you're clearly not okay with this, and I don't want to make you uncomfortable."

Her eyes lock onto mine, and I wish I knew what she was thinking.

"I'm fine. I promise. I just …" She shifts her gaze to the bed. "I thought we had two beds." Her gaze moves to the couch.

Maybe that's not a bad solution. I pick up a cushion.

"Not a pullout."

"Of course it's not."

My eyes find hers again. "Last chance. I can go get my own room, or we share a bed."

Because the world has decided to punish me, she bites her bottom lip, then quickly lets it go with a pop. "We share."

"Alright, do you—"

"I also suggest we entertain the idea of a possible truce this weekend in honor of my brothers and Sadie."

"A truce?"

"Yes." She nods as if it's settled. "No arguing this weekend."

I grin and then cross my arms.

"I think that's going to be easier for me than it will be for you."

She points at me.

"Because you say things like that."

"I think you like it when I say things like this."

"I don't."

"You do."

She smiles and I wink at her.

"Alright, fine. Let's just … relax for the next two days."

"I can do that," I tell her.

"Good."

"Yeah."

"What should we do first?"

"Well"—I twist to look around the room.—"what do you do in your free time?"

"I don't have any."

"Fair."

"You?"

I chuckle. "It's not appropriate for this conversation."

"We're both adults."

True.

"I'd probably get off."

Silence follows.

"I walked into that one, didn't I?" she asks.

"Yeah."

"Cool." She perks up and then marches to her bag and opens it.

"I'm going to take my things and get ready with Grace and Brooke."

"You're sure?"

"Yes," she says and is out the door in the next minute.

———

THE BATHROOM SINK is running when I come back to the room a couple of hours later.

With Ruby gone, I'd taken the free time to meet Linc and Dutton downstairs for a drink and to gamble a little before we needed to change and meet the others for dinner.

"I'm back," I announce so that I don't freak her out when she realizes she's not alone anymore.

"Okay," she shouts back through the bathroom door. "I need about five more minutes."

"I'm going to change then."

"Sounds good."

I change quickly, add some deodorant and cologne, and take a seat on the couch to wait for her.

Every thought stops when Ruby walks out of the bathroom.

I don't know what I was expecting, but it wasn't for my heart to pound the way it is right now.

I wasn't expecting my brain to become obsessed with her the way it is at this moment.

Obsessed.

Addicted.

Both are accurate to describe the way my eyes are glued to her and my palms are growing sweaty.

It's not a good look for me, but fuck.

Wow.

Although she maxes out at five foot five, those black heels make her slim legs look as if they go for miles. Not to mention where the emerald dress ends above her upper thigh.

Hell, if she turns around, I'm not so sure it's going to cover her ass.

As if she can read my mind, she turns to duck back into the bathroom for something, and sure as shit, it barely covers her backside.

It's backless with thin gold straps holding it up. I groan.

I don't know what I was expecting for tonight, but this was not it.

"Do I look okay?" she asks. "You're looking at me all weird."

I nod.

"Yeah. Yeah," is all I manage to choke out.

Her brows dip as she glares at me.

My response is clearly not the one she wanted, but I'm not so sure she would care for the one I want to give her.

"Thanks," she says.

I clear my throat and pull myself together.

"What I meant to say was, you look nice, Ruby."

"Nice," she repeats. "Nice?"

"Yes, nice."

She pops one hip to her side and rests her hand on it. She freezes with a huff for a split second before shaking her head and moving for the door.

"Nice is not the look I was going for."

She passes me, grabbing her clutch off the little table near the door.

"What look were you going for?"

Another huff as she tosses her hands up.

"Honestly, I don't know, but maybe one that's a bit more sexy than nice. No one wants to touch *nice*."

I pause to process what she just said and to think over my next words carefully.

She wants a look that screams *touch me*. Is that what she said?

How is that …

What does she …

My thoughts jumble in my mind and before I know it, I'm saying the one that is bound to shock her the most.

"You want to be touched, Ruby? Is that what you're telling me?"

"I—" Her green eyes focus on me, and I can tell right away that she's just now realizing what she said out loud. "Yes."

I move closer to her. I tell myself it's because she's by the door and we need to leave to meet the others, but right now my body wants nothing more than to be close to hers.

"I can assure you," I say when I'm right in front of her, "that as long as you are with me, there will not be another man laying a single fucking finger on you."

She sucks in a breath, her chest lifting and drawing my gaze to the dip in the front of her dress.

"Won't that defeat the purpose of what I just said?" she asks.

Slowly, I drag my eyes back to hers.

Her lips part, and I'm tempted to kiss her right here, right now, and change the plans of our entire night.

"I said another man won't be laying a finger on you, not that no man would."

She doesn't miss a beat.

"So that man will be you?"

Her words come out all breathy, and the want in them leaves me growing hard in my pants.

"Do you want that man to be me?"

I wait with bated breath for her answer, my body drawing close to hers as she looks at my mouth.

But then someone pounds on the door, and we both jump.

"Ruby, Declan, are you ready?"

Ruby closes her eyes and tucks away from me, so I let out a breath and open the door.

"Luca, yes, we are ready."

"Waiting at the door, I guess." He laughs then heads down the hall to meet the others.

I hold the door open wider for Ruby to walk through, my eyes drifting to every inch of her backside.

The rest of the group is waiting by the elevators. The vibe hits me instantly, and I let out a little laugh. Ruby must feel it, too, but instead of laughing, she just outright calls it as it is.

"Oh, great. You're all going to be alpha fiancés and enjoy zero percent of the night because of what the girls are wearing, aren't you?"

"Well, I sure as shit don't want other guys thinking what I'm thinking," Luca says, sending a look of warning to Shay.

She smiles, pressing to her toes to kiss his lips.

"Agreed," Miles says, hooking his arm around Quinn and pulling her close.

"Let's all just be smart tonight, okay?" Hudson adds.

Ruby shakes her head. "I'm hearing a lot of talking, but none of you have said the right thing."

I chuckle louder.

"Ladies, you all look stunning tonight," I say to lighten the mood.

"And that right there is what each of you should have said." Ruby points to her brothers one by one. "Each. Of. You."

All three of them grumble an apology to their girls, and when Ruby is satisfied, she steps in front of me to hit the elevator button, my eyes dropping again to her where her dress ends dangerously just over her ass.

A throat clears next to me.

I startle and look to my right.

Luca has his arms crossed as he glares at me.

He mouths, "Be smart."

I smile and give him a thumbs-up.

Too late for that warning.

———

THE CLUB IS in full swing by the time we finish dinner and make it back to the hotel. Truth be told, it's 11 P.M. and I could go to sleep, but according to Hudson's hockey friends, this is the time you go to the club—even then, we are arriving early.

I glance around the group as Hudson and his hockey friends speak with the guy who determines who gets to go inside the club and who will wait in line.

No one seems to be tired, and the girls actually look excited.

After all, the one thing Sadie asked for was to go to a "club

club," which she defined as not just a bar with dancing, but a full-blown stage and booths and bottle service.

How she came up with this idea, I have no idea.

"I can't believe we are doing this," Ruby says, leaning into me. "This is everything the opposite of our small-town life."

Maybe that's why Sadie wanted a club night.

"You got that right."

"Did you go to clubs while you lived in Chicago?"

Her question takes me by surprise. Ruby can talk a lot, but her inquiry about my past away from Lovers isn't her normal go-to conversation.

"No. Not once."

I glance down at her just as she looks up.

"Really?"

"Really." I nod.

"You never wanted to?"

I shrug. "It wasn't like I hated the idea. I'm actually curious to see how all of this works, but it's not me."

"I feel the same way."

Hudson waves a hand to grab our attention and the group starts to follow.

We walk right by a long line of eager partiers.

I make eye contact with a few of them, mostly women, all harmless.

But then someone whistles and shouts, "Yeah, Green, let me see that ass."

My entire body freezes.

Who the fuck talks like that?

I spin to find the voice and see a man rubbing his chin and licking his lips.

I move for him, but Ruby grabs my arm.

"Don't."

"He can't talk to you like that."

"No, he can't, but I'm never going to see that man again, so I'm going to let it go and enjoy the night with my friends."

"What if he makes it into the club and seeks you out, then he tries to grab you and—"

"Whoa, whoa, turn off dad mode, please, and give me just Declan Young, Ruby's friend for the night."

She grabs my hand and drags me to where the others are waiting, clearly oblivious to what just happened.

I follow but look over my shoulder to glare at the man again.

I see you, asshole. I won't forget that face.

We all squeeze into an elevator that has its own escort. The motion jerks so fast that Ruby stumbles, steadying when she bumps her ass into my junk and my hand slides around to her stomach to hold her still.

Because I feel I need to make this clear now, I lean forward to whisper in her ear.

"For the record, Declan Young would never let a man like that talk to his *friends*. Once we are back in Lovers, you might go back to hating me, but hating me or not, you deserve fucking respect from every single person who meets you. End of story."

Her chest rises and falls quickly.

I lean a little closer.

"Did you hear me, Ruby?"

She nods.

"Good."

We reach the floor of the club and file out. Like many moments before this one, the group walks in pairs of two.

Instead of waiting to be the last ones, Ruby grabs my hand and falls into line.

She tugs me close and says, "Just to be sure about that guy, how about you stick with me tonight?"

I slide a hand around her hips, and because it's loud as fuck in here, I place my lips right next to her ear. "I was planning on it."

CHAPTER SEVENTEEN

RUBY

Time seems to stop when you're having fun, and right now, I can't remember the last time I had this much fun that didn't include my son.

Hudson opted for a table with bottle service. I can't even begin to think of what something like this would cost. We have our own half-circle booth that fits all of us, with room to spare. There is a table in front of the seating with a cutout in the middle for ice and drinks. There are bottles of three different alcohols and the juice or beverage of choice to mix with them and a dedicated waitress who has been here the entire time to make our drinks.

Even though I haven't drunk anything but water, my mind is blown that people experience this more than once in their lives.

A Bar Song by Shaboozy is playing, and the girls and I have huddled together as we dance and shake and sing as loudly as we can. Not that anyone can hear us over the volume of the music and club noise in general. The guys are sitting down and seem to be deep into multiple conversations. When random songs come on, a few will come to dance with us.

Mostly Hudson, Luca, and Miles. Dutton and Linc wandered off with Carver and Archer a while ago, and we haven't seen them since.

The next song bleeds into the ending of the current one, never letting the music stop.

Shay yawns, leaving the girls to find my brother.

She whispers in his ear, and then Hudson and Miles nod quickly.

Declan's eyes are already on me.

I've sneaked glances at him all night, and every time I've caught him looking back.

At some point, I'd assumed he would dance with me the way the others did, but he never moved.

He just watched.

Me.

Only me.

Knowing he can't take his eyes off me has kept my body alive all night.

"We're going to head back to the room," Hudson leans in to yell into my ear. He jerks his thumb over his shoulder in case I couldn't hear him.

I spot the others in the group gathering any belongings they brought and a different waitress steps up to Hudson with a little clipboard.

My brother signs it, and then the group moves for the door, but Declan's hand grabs mine.

"We should stay," he says.

"Yes," I answer without thinking.

The group keeps moving, but Luca looks over his shoulder and gives me a thumbs-up.

I return it and then spin to find Declan talking to the waitress.

He holds a finger up and then slips a hand around my middle to pull me close.

"Do you want to keep this table or move to the dance floor?" he asks.

"What do you want to do?"

His eyes lock onto mine as a smirk touches his lips.

"I want to dance with you."

I pinch my lips together to hold back the mega smile that wants to take over.

"Okay."

He waves to the waitress and then pulls me to the dance floor.

It's packed, body to body, and as soon as Declan finds a spot he likes, there isn't an inch of space left between us.

His hands remain on my hips, and I rest mine around his neck.

The move is old school as hell, but I sway my body back and forth to the music and close my eyes, letting this moment engrave itself into my memories. Declan spins me, my back to his front. His hand comes around to my stomach, and I back up slightly. The moment my ass grinds into him, he tugs me tighter to his body.

I feel him harden instantly.

It only makes my body melt into his and into the music even more.

Right now, I'm not Ruby the mom who got pregnant as a teen. I'm just Ruby, a woman dancing with a man in a nightclub and having fun.

I spin in his arms to face him, opening my eyes and they lock onto Declan's instantly.

I want to ask him what he's thinking.

Ask him why he wanted to stay with just me.

Or why everything between us feels different now and how did it happen so easily?

I want to know the answer to things that would only compli-cate my life.

So I don't ask any of them.

What I really want is to kiss him and for him to kiss me back.

My gaze shifts to his lips, and I swear my hand acts on its own, threading my fingers up his neck and into his hair, pulling him closer.

He doesn't fight it, and it only intensifies this pull that's happening between us.

His nose touches mine and I tilt my chin up.

I want him to take that last little inch. I want him to make that call.

"Ruby," he says in that deep tone that sends goosebumps over my skin. It's a mix of need and warning. "I can't let our first kiss be in the middle of a dance floor in a club."

My heart pounds.

"Where do you want it to be?"

The words have barely left my mouth before he's pulling me off the floor that we just stepped out onto and through the pathway to the exit doors. We stop in a darkened hallway that muffles the music and we're completely alone.

Quickly, Declan leans me into the wall and presses himself into me.

His lips touch my neck, my jaw, and my entire body relaxes.

It's been far too long since I've had a man kiss me. Anywhere.

"The first time we kiss should be for us and just us," he says. "I don't like to share, Ruby."

My entire body tingles at his confession.

Is Declan possessive?

My nipples harden.

I hope he is.

"We're alone now," I whisper, and he groans.

He nips at my bottom lip. I mimic his hands and clutch his sides, pulling him into me.

I've never wanted to be touched by someone the way I want Declan to touch me right now.

Like if he doesn't kiss me, or more, soon, I'll combust.

"Kiss me. Please."

"There is no going back after this," he says.

"I know."

"And you still want it?"

I nod.

"I need words, Ruby."

"Yes, I want it. I want you."

"Good answer," he says.

His hand slides up the front of my dress, between my breasts and up my neck, then grips my chin.

Our eyes meet for the briefest of moments before he kisses me.

Pressing his mouth to mine with command.

I kiss him back on a moan and something in that makes him snap. His hands move to my ass now, gripping it tightly as he slips his tongue into my mouth, then he switches the angle to kiss me deeper.

His hands slide to my thighs, and he picks me up.

I wrap my legs around him, and with the next dance of his tongue against mine, I wrap my arms around his neck to hold on.

"Fuck," he says, breaking his kiss and pressing his lips to my shoulders.

Then his lips are on mine again.

He keeps me pressed to the wall, sneaking a hand between us and touching me between the legs.

"Oh God." I let my head drop back to the wall.

His mouth goes to my neck again; his finger tugs my panties to the side.

"Shit," someone yells, and it breaks the spell.

Delcan sets me to my feet in an instant and backs up.

Chests heaving for air, we look right and then left.

Not a single person in sight.

I touch a hand to my lips.

I almost forgot we're at a club.

I'd laugh if the look in Declan's eyes weren't so dark.

"We're leaving," he says. "Now."

———

THE DOOR to our hotel room closes, and I swear the air in the room thickens. As if it knows that lines are about to be crossed and no matter what is said or done in here tonight, we can't go back.

I don't want to go back.

I want to be here and now and let whatever happens tonight stay here.

In Vegas.

I step farther into the room, but Declan grabs my hand and pulls me back.

With my front pressed to his, his hand that isn't holding my waist now moves to my neck.

He gently tips my head back, and as if I were in my very own romance novel, he groans.

I'm beginning to grow addicted to that noise.

"Your skin is so soft."

Then he drops a featherlight kiss just under my jaw.

"I knew it would be."

He quickly licks the side of my face, then blows on it, sending chills and goosebumps over my skin.

His lips are on mine before I have time to form a thought.

His tongue wastes no time slipping into my mouth and deepening the kiss.

I let out a mew of relief.

Suddenly, he spins, pinning me between him and the door, pressing himself into me just like he did at the club.

He's hard.

I knew he would be, but right now I'm getting a better idea of just how big he actually is, and it's a lot bigger than I remember from the couch.

Eager to know the truth, I let a hand slide between us and begin to unbuckle his belt.

He doesn't try to stop me. He simply keeps kissing me and gliding his hands over my body.

When I get the belt loose and flick open his pants, he pauses, both hands on my body.

"I need you to tell me that you're positive you want this."

"I'm positive, but it has to stay here. In Vegas. We can't do this when we get home."

His gaze lands on mine, heated and needy.

He nods slightly. "Okay, but we're sober, baby. You won't have an excuse to regret this in the morning."

His grip on my hips tightens.

I'd assumed he wasn't drinking but didn't know for sure until this moment.

The persona he shows in his everyday life, the soft, gentle girl dad who is nerdy and always ready to help everyone else is gone, and in his place is a man who is ready to snap as soon as he has the green light to take what he wants.

And he wants me.

And I want him even more.

And I have a feeling there won't be anything soft or gentle about this with him.

I close my eyes and tilt my head back on a groan. The motion presses my waistline against his.

When I open my eyes again, I make sure his are locked on mine. I need him to hear me loud and clear and stop talking so he can ruin me.

Because I know he will.

"The only thing I regret is not letting this happen sooner. Now, kiss me and take my clothes off. Please."

The word falls from my lips as desperate begging.

"Jesus," he whispers.

We reach the bed, and the vibe he gives me says he's going to toss me on it, but he doesn't. He dips slowly to lay me back, one arm across my lower back so that he can move me to the center of the bed.

His lips find my neck and then my chest, and then he's slowly peeling the straps of my dress over my shoulder.

My skin burns under his touch with a need I've never felt before.

"Just rip it off, Declan," I say in a tone I didn't know I had.

It's desperate.

"And miss watching the way you come undone when I touch you? No."

His hands glide over my shoulders, and I let out a whine that I'm not proud of.

"Please," I beg again.

"I have a question for you."

"Now?" I huff.

"Yes," he says and lifts my hips to pull my dress off.

"Fine. What?"

"When you said *dry spell* in your text, how long has it been since someone other than you or your vibrators got you off?"

My first thought is to argue once more that he read my text, but my body knows that the sooner I give him what he wants, the sooner he will give me what I want.

"Six years," I answer.

He stops.

"Six years," he repeats.

I can't decipher the look in his eyes, but it makes me cross my arms in front of my body to hide.

"No, don't do that," he says quickly and pulls himself together. "I didn't mean to freeze like that. I just … six years?"

"Can you stop saying that?"

"I — How is that possible?"

"Because it is. I don't sleep around. I've only ever been with Max's dad and—"

"Stop." His head drops, and he presses his eyes closed so hard, I see a crinkle at the edge of them.

I scoot up and grab my dress.

The moment is clearly ruined now.

"Sorry, I didn't—"

"Don't apologize," he says.

"You don't even know what I was going to apologize for."

"Exactly. Nothing at this moment requires an apology from you."

"But I ruined … this."

He finally looks up at me, and a soft smile touches his lips.

"No, baby, you didn't. You just reminded me how lucky I am that you're letting me in this way."

"Oh. So, you still want me?"

"Fuck yes, I do."

I bite my lip.

"Okay."

He leans forward and kisses me, slowly laying his body over mine. I relax back into the bed, and he adjusts us, allowing his body to rest between my legs.

Everything about his touch is gentler now.

"I won't break, Declan."

"I know, but I might."

His lips continue to make their way down my body.

He reaches my underwear and pulls them off, now kissing his way up my inner thigh.

This man is determined to put his lips against every part of my body before the night is over.

As he gets closer and closer to my core, I begin to fidget. When he's one kiss away, I reach for him and try to pull him up.

He looks up with a question in his eyes.

"You're joking, right?"

I shake my head.

"Fuck," he says on a growl and then jerks my body to his fast as he drops to his knees off the bed and licks me slowly up the middle.

"Ohhhh!" I jerk up.

"Lie down," he says with command and pushes me back, keeping his arm there to hold me down.

His tongue begins to flick faster and faster, and when he sucks on my clit, I cry out. I didn't know I could make that sound.

"You're so fucking sweet, Ruby," he says quickly before diving back in.

Once he gets a rhythm, my hands find his hair, and I tug gently.

"Yes," I moan and then run my hands through my own hair.

I can feel the sensation building, and my heart starts to race.

"Declan," I whimper and reach down to touch myself.

He smacks my hand away, keeping his eyes on mine as he slides a finger inside of me, his thumb rubbing my clit now.

"You're beautiful," he says, moving to lie next to me, adding a finger and pressing his lips to mine.

I have this urge to freak out, given where his mouth just was, but I don't have the chance to before my entire body starts to convulse.

I let out a long breath and multiple short ones. Declan captures each one with a kiss.

When my orgasm ends and my body is still buzzing with bliss, I open my eyes.

His smile instantly warms me, and I relax into his arms.

I twist a little to kiss him, brushing my hand against his erection.

I grin and slowly grip him.

"Shit," he hisses.

"Was that too tight?" I jerk my hand back.

He laughs.

"Jesus, you're too innocent for me."

"I am not," I snap.

"Oh, I could argue that."

"I'm not innocent," I repeat and take him in my hand again.

I start with slow strokes, keeping my grip firm but not too hard.

I stroke down and then up, letting my thumb sweep over the tip.

He groans and leans back to rest against the bed.

I smirk and then bend down and take him in my mouth.

"Holy fuck," he almost shouts. "Oh God."

With my lips wrapped around him, I take him as far down as I can until I feel him touch the back of my throat.

"Ruby," he growls.

I take that as a good sign and keep going. My hand pumping and my mouth sucking.

Harder.

Faster.

His hips start to match my rhythm, and my confidence boosts.

Now probably isn't the time to tell him I've never done this before either, but I have read books and seen movies, so I'm going off research that has clearly proven right.

"I'm about to come," he announces and tries to pull me up.

I don't let him.

I'm too into it now.

Too into the way I have him at my mercy, and I'm not letting up.

Hand and mouth in sync now, I move faster until I feel the warmth of his release on my tongue.

I swallow every last bit of it.

When I finally come up for air, Declan is breathing hard and staring at me.

"Was that innocent enough for you?"

He lets out a bark of a laugh and pulls me to him.

"Not even a little."

"Good." I smile and relax into his arms.

I'm closing my eyes when I spot the clock by the side of the bed.

"Holy shit, it's 5:30 in the morning. We are going to be worthless tomorrow if we don't go to bed now."

"And it was worth every moment."

CHAPTER EIGHTEEN

DECLAN

The rest of the group beats us to the pool the next morning. It makes sense, given that Ruby and I stayed up after them and then some.

Fuck.

I can't keep the smile off my face.

I spot the group quickly. There are two loungers saved for us under a cabana. The only downside is that they aren't next to each other. Ruby's is on the other side of Sadie; mine is between Luca and Dutton.

Ruby's walking in front of me in a blue bikini, and it's taking all I have not to just stare at her. To let my eyes leisurely take her in with memories of the way she fell apart for me last night.

Six years.

Shit.

And he never went down on her.

Idiot.

No wonder they didn't make it.

Not that sex is the reason people should be together, but hell.

Ruby is basically a virgin again.

It took all I had not to just fuck her last night.

I chose to ease her into it, and let me tell you, I don't know if I can do that again tonight.

She's stunning, and now that I know what her body looks like under that cover-up, and now that I know how soft her skin feels under my fingers, how she tastes between her legs, and the sounds she makes when she comes, all I want to do is give her orgasm after orgasm.

Hell, I was with Susie's mother for years, and not once did I crave her the way I crave Ruby right now. It hit me the moment we woke up this morning. I was tempted to reach for her, to kiss her and repeat all of last night, but Ruby simply woke up, asked me if I wanted coffee, made me a cup, and then she got in the shower as if it were any other morning.

I thought about joining her, but we both missed dozens of texts from the group. We couldn't be any later than we already were.

We also didn't talk about it.

Not one single word.

As if everything between us didn't change last night.

Ruby pauses, looking left and right.

"They're over there," I say, pointing to the group and brushing my hand to the small of her back to guide her in the right direction.

"Oh wow, how could I miss them? They take up so much space."

I chuckle.

"This place is pretty packed already."

"Yeah. I'm glad they were able to save us spots."

I don't tell her that I wish they were next to each other. Or how I wish someone would suggest a free day so I can find an excuse to be alone with Ruby again. Waiting for everyone to leave last night was pure agony.

In our room or in public, I don't care. I just want to be alone with her. She relaxed when it was just us in the club last night, and I want her to know that this Ruby should come out more often. That she doesn't have to be "on" all the time. She has her family and me, and we've got her back so she can have fun, too.

But at the same time, I know what it's like to be the default parent. The one who is responsible for everything and has to be on their A game at all times.

I'm not saying Ruby and I should get married and parent together, but I am saying she can count on me. Even when she didn't care for me, I'd have been there if she needed me.

I just need to find a way to show her, because coming right out to say it won't click the same way.

Ruby is a woman who needs to see action. I'm starting to see that words, for her, mean nothing without it.

We reach the group, and Ruby just walks away from me as if it were any other day.

I let out a breath and then drop my towel onto the chair next to Lucas. I sit, lay back, and cross my arms.

"Oh, someone is grumpy today," Luca says. "How late did you and Ruby stay out?"

"We got back to the room around four."

I think.

Linc, on the other side of Luca, leans forward. "Was it just you two?"

I nod. I open my mouth to ask him where he disappeared to, but he beats me to it.

"How did that go?"

I shrug. "Fine."

"You got along okay?" Dutton asks.

I nod again.

"You two have been getting along a lot better lately. Living together and now sharing a room…" His sentence lingers in the air.

I know what he's implying, and he's not wrong. His time-frame of when it started might be, but yeah.

"Oh, no, you're not denying it this time," Linc says in a whisper.

Luca just stares at me, and Dutton chuckles behind me.

"I … it's not like that. I told you. We are becoming friends. That's all."

Fuck is it ever.

Shay walks by, and Luca jumps up.

He points at me. "This conversation isn't over." Then he follows Shay to wherever she's headed.

Whatever happens in Vegas stays in Vegas. While she didn't say those exact words, that was Ruby's mindset last night, and she's not wrong to have it.

There is no way I can go back to Lovers and not touch her again, knowing what I know now, but I have to. My focus needs to be on finalizing this deal. Distractions mean delay, and delay means … old habits that I never want to see again.

I know myself well enough to know how easily I could forget the goal and repeat the past. As I said before, Ruby deserves actions, and once this deal is done, I can give them to her.

Her and Susie both.

Not to mention the connection she and Max have to my competition.

It seems cleaner if we keep this to just the weekend.

But we still have another night here, so I'm not done with her yet.

The hairs on the back of my neck tingle. Ruby is looking right at me.

She bites her bottom lip and then smirks, slowly moving her

attention back to the girls. Grace's hands are waving about a mile a minute as she tells whatever story she has going on.

Fuck.

Finally, a reaction that Ruby didn't forget last night.

"Whoa, earth to Declan." Dutton waves a hand in front of my face.

"What?"

"You can't deny anything is going on between you and Ruby and then stare at her just minutes later the way you were right now."

"I wasn't looking at her in any sort of way."

Linc moves to Luca's seat. He swings his legs over to my side and leans closer to me, his forearms on top of his knees.

"You're looking at her the way Hudson would look at my sister back when they denied it, too. I know the signs this time around." He shakes his head. "You are crushing on your friend's sister and denying it. Bold and bad move, man."

"I … it's complicated."

"I knew this was going to happen." Dutton is now mimicking Linc's position, and I'm still just lying back on my lounger between them. "I knew there was no way you two could live together and not start something. I mean, if I can feel the tension between you, it has to be electric at home. Then I saw you last night at the club and—"

"You saw us?" I snap up and look at Dutton. "When?"

"When I sure as shit shouldn't have seen you. I'll deny it if you tell anyone, but I think you two are a good match."

Linc and I are both silent as Dutton nods.

Is he … smiling?

Does Dutton smile?

"Are you okay?" I ask. You know, to be sure.

"Yeah, why?"

"You're …"

"Smiling," Linc finishes for me.

"Ah, fuck you guys. I smile." Then he leans back, tucking both hands behind his head. "Especially when I'm on vacation and have nothing to worry about except what I'm going to eat or drink next."

Linc chuckles and then relaxes, too.

A waitress comes by, and just as I order a cold water, my phone rings with a FaceTime from my parents.

"Be right back," I say and then hold the phone up. "Hello," I say with a grin as Susie's face fills the screen.

"Dad!" she cheers and then, "Ruby!"

I twist to see Ruby right behind me, crowding my space to get into the picture. Her hand falls to my shoulder, and she settles in at my side.

"Hey, girl, is Max with you?"

"Max!"

Suddenly, the screen is filled with two grinning faces.

"You're at the pool!" Max points out, and Susie sticks her bottom lip out.

"Without us?"

"You two were at the lake all day yesterday," we hear Colt say in the background. "And as soon as you finish lunch, we are going back."

He pops onto the screen to wave.

My parents do the same.

"Is that Ruby? Let me see," my mom yells from the background and leans into view of the camera. "Oh, wow, you are gorgeous, dear."

"Mom," I scold as she and the kids all try to be the main focus of the camera.

Ruby giggles.

"What?" Mom says. "Are you having fun?"

"We are," I answer for both of us.

"Good. You needed time for yourselves."

I share a look with Ruby, and she blushes.

There is a rustle on the other end and then the phone drops.

I love FaceTiming with my kid, but her attention span is short.

Colt grabs the phone. "And we are on to the next activity."

"Are they behaving?" I ask.

He nods. "These two are something else." He laughs. "But I love it. Go have fun. Stop worrying about us here."

"Okay," Ruby says quickly. "Bye."

Then she ducks back to the group.

"Huh," Colt says. "She was quick with that."

"Yeah." I look over my shoulder at her and hear Colt laugh.

"What?"

"Nothing," Then he clears his throat. "Just make sure she has fun, alright?"

I nod. "I'll make sure of it."

When I get back to my seat, everyone is packing up.

"We're leaving? We just got here."

"No, *you* just got here," Miles says. "We have been here for hours."

As he packs his bag, he gives me two glances.

Does he know something?

"Let's all meet up for dinner," Hudson suggests and looks around the group as if he needs confirmation.

At this point, whatever he or Sadie says goes.

"Meet in the lobby?" I offer.

"Great," he says and then swings his arm around Sadie before guiding her into the hotel. Like always, each couple follows suit. And just like last night, it leaves Ruby and I alone.

I don't mind this theme anymore.

"Not going in?" I ask.

She grins, relaxing back even more into her lounge.

"I have three hours to not be needed anywhere; I'm staying right here to soak up the sun for just a little bit more."

I nod, then glance around.

"Care for some company?"

"Only if it's you."

"I'd fight for this spot," I tell her, earning me a bigger smile.

"So, is your mind saying *sit here for three hours*, or is there something else you want to do?"

She doesn't answer right away, but she does turn her head slowly to me.

"I'm not sure. I don't get this opportunity very often. Not for long periods of time, anyway."

I know bits and pieces of Ruby's past before she came back to Lovers, but it's all hearsay. Before this trip, I don't think she would have ever sat down to talk to me about it, but she might now.

"You didn't have free time before you moved back?"

"Some, but I felt guilty every single time someone was watching Max just so I could do something I wanted alone. Like I was a bad mom for enjoying even a half hour without him."

I reach for her hand, lacing my own with hers.

She allows it.

"I know it won't help, but nothing about that is true. You're a fantastic mom, Ruby. You deserve to still be you on top of being a mom."

"I know, and I tell myself that all the time, but it just doesn't seem to click."

"Are you feeling guilty now?"

She shrugs. "A little. Max would be over the moon for this pool."

I chuckle. "Susie would, too."

"We'll have to bring them sometime because they would love everything about the lights on the Strip, too."

"Bring them together?" I ask in a teasing tone.

"I —oh, I didn't mean it like … shoot." She quickly swings her legs over the side of the lounger and pulls her hand from mine. "I don't think, like, since you, you know, put your face between my legs that means we are together or anything. That would be silly, and I made a rule last night and you agreed to it, and I'm not crazy, but, I mean, if you want to do that again, I won't stop you, but oh my God, it's not required, and why aren't you cutting me off to stop this rambling?"

I mirror her position and cup the side of her face, my thumb brushing her bottom lip. She leans into it and glances up at me.

"I like when you ramble," I admit to her. "I'm used to short quick quips from you, so hearing you talk more? I like it."

She rolls her eyes. "If you're just trying to say cute stuff to get me back into the bed we are sharing, you can stop. Even if I wanted to resist you, my body wouldn't let me."

"Is that so?"

She nods.

"Just your body?"

I lean a little closer, angling my head to kiss her.

"Yes."

"Hmm." I press a soft kiss to her lips.

This is what I wanted after we woke up. Just a small moment with her to tell me I'm not crazy. What happened between us, she felt it, too.

She pops back quickly, her focus darting over my shoulder.

I practically snap my neck to see who she is looking at, but I don't see anyone we know.

I turn back around just in time for her to grab my face.

"It's all clear."

Then she presses her lips to mine, climbing into my lap. With one leg on each side of mine, she threads her hands in my hair and deepens the kiss.

The splashing of water reminds us where we are. I break the kiss, and she slinks back to her seat as if she'd forgotten, too.

"We could go get something to eat," I suggest and Ruby hums.

"Burgers?"

I nod. "Milkshakes?"

"Yesss."

For the next three hours, once we change into day clothes, Ruby and I eat, overdose on sweet treats, and walk the Strip.

She's a completely different woman than the one back home, and truth be told, I'm into them both. But this version of Ruby lets me kiss her anytime I want.

———

THE TEXT MESSAGES start about twenty minutes before we are supposed to meet everyone downstairs.

LUCA:

Shay isn't feeling well. We are staying in.

HUDSON:

Sadie and I were just talking about how neither of us feel very well. I think we are, too.

MILES:

Thank God you all mentioned it first. I didn't want to be the one to bail. This is Vegas after all. Who gets sick in Vegas?

LINC:

Was it the all-you-can-eat fish breakfast bar?

DECLAN:

When did you eat that?

HUDSON:

While you and Ruby were still sleeping.

DUTTON:

It had to be. It's why we're all sick right now.

DECLAN:

I'm not sick.

A string of middle finger emojis takes over, so I set my phone down.

"How does this look?" Ruby says, stepping out of the bathroom in nothing but her red thong, matching bra, and black heels. Her makeup is done, and her hair is pulled up high with some pieces falling down around her face. "Too much?"

I nod and move toward her.

"Way too much. Take it off. All of it."

I reach for her, but she laughs, pushing me away with a hand to my chest.

"Nope. Stop. We will never make it out of this room if you keep this up."

Which is exactly why we spent the day away from the room. I had the same thought.

I put both hands on her hips and pull her to me, kissing down her neck.

"It's a good thing that the rest of the group has food poisoning and is staying in for the night, leaving us to do whatever we want."

Because what I want doesn't involve clothes, and this view right now is a good sign that she's thinking about it, too.

She gasps.

"What?"

I slide my phone from my back pocket and show her the texts.

"Oh no, let me check my phone. I bet the girls have sent something, too."

It's pure torture for me to watch her practically glide around the room in nothing but her underwear.

"Oh yeah, Sadie is sick, so is Shay. Quinn says she's fine, but Miles isn't doing too well. Grace says she's not so bad, but since Brooke is down for the count too, she has already gotten on the laptop to check work emails."

"Sooo …"

"I guess it's just us."

I snap my fingers.

"Shame."

Ruby blushes and gravitates into my arms.

I press my lips to hers, and she moans into my mouth.

I take one hand to cup her breast, squeezing gently until her hips press into me.

"I guess we can stay in, too," she says on a breath.

I grip her ass with one hand and smooth the other down the front of her panties, finally giving in to what I've wanted all day long.

"Oh, hell, Ruby. Is this all because you're thinking of me?"

She nods. "And your hands and your mouth—eep!"

I toss her onto the bed, catching her by the ankles.

I hold them together and look at her wide eyes. "We're not staying in tonight."

"We're not?" Her bottom lip pops out with her question.

"Nope. I'm taking you out."

"Like … on a date?"

"Exactly like on a date."

"Well," she says, "then this part happens after."

I lean forward, stopping her exit.

"Before and after, and after again is preferred. I won't be able to show you a proper time if I'm obsessing over this."

She grins.

"Now lay back down and spread your legs. I'm not leaving this room until you've come at least twice. Got it?"

"Yes, sir."

I groan.

"Who knew you could be such a good *good* girl for me?"

Her chest rises on a breath and she blows it out slowly, doing exactly as I asked.

I unbutton my shirt, strip it over my head, and then remove my pants, all while never taking my eyes off her.

This side of Ruby is for my eyes only, and I'll be damned if I'm not going to make sure she knows it.

Should I wait until after dinner for this? Probably. But if we wait, I have no doubt that the two of us will be rushing to get back to the room, ready to continue what we started last night.

I don't want that.

I mean, I do.

But I meant what I said earlier.

I want to make sure she has fun.

Both in the room and out of it.

I want to take my time, the way I did last night, but it seems Ruby has other plans.

She grabs my face and kisses me, her body pressing into mine until I lie on my back. She climbs on top of me, straddling me and grinding her hips until it isn't possible for me to get harder.

"I wanted this last night," she says, leaning forward to kiss my chest. "So please don't make me wait this time."

"I won't." I flip her onto her back.

I press my cock into her core with force and then pull back to remove her panties.

Once they are gone, I take a finger and run it up her slick folds.

Then I stick those fingers into my mouth and suck.

"So. Fucking. Sweet."

On her next inhale, I slide that same finger back inside of her and then get on my knees.

Pulsing my finger, I begin to lick at her wetness.

Her hips buck, and my cock twitches at how responsive she is to me.

I feel her start to tighten around me, and withdraw my fingers, replacing them with the tip of my cock.

She instantly sits up, her focus settling on where we meet.

"You want to watch?" I ask.

She nods.

"I don't have a condom."

"I can see that. I'm clean."

"Me too."

"Then what are you waiting for?"

Her eagerness turns me on even more, and I press into her.

"Oh fuck," she purrs on a breath, her head falling back for a split moment before she brings her gaze back to us.

I push in more, and she lifts her ass.

For someone who doesn't have much experience, she sure as hell knows what she likes.

Suddenly, the image of her vibrators comes into my mind.

She's known what she likes for a long time now.

She just needs to be reminded of how much better it is with a real person.

I grab her hips and slam into her.

Holy fuck, she's tight.

So tight, I have to stall my movements to pull myself together. If I come too soon, she will most likely have an old man joke for me, and I don't think I could take that right now.

"I can't believe it fits," she says on a breath. "You feel … so … good."

I smirk, pulling out slowly only to thrust back in.

"Baby, I wish I could describe how you feel right now. Tight. Hot. Wet. Those only begin to explain it."

I press all the way in again, swivel my hips, and she moans.

"I want it hard, Declan."

I'm not so sure she knows what she's asking.

"Declan, did you hear me?"

I nod.

"Then fuck me harder."

I stop then, my gaze laser focused on hers.

"That's what you want?"

"Yes."

In one swift movement, I flip her over and pull her ass up until she's on her knees and slam back into her.

"Ah!" she screams.

Maybe that was too much.

"Again, Declan."

I do it again.

And again

And again.

Fucking her as fast and hard as I can.

When she plants her hands and pushes back toward me, I slap her ass so hard, my palms sting.

Her body convulses around me, and the suction of her pussy releases me instantly.

I pull out and stroke myself as I come all over her back.

Breathing heavily, I fall to my back next to her.

She rests on her stomach, turning her face to look at mine.

Then she smiles.

"That was perfect. Thank you."

Her politeness cracks me up.

"You're welcome."

I lean forward, kiss her lips, and then jump up to clean myself and get her a washcloth.

Once I've cleaned myself off her, we finally get ready and head out for a night on the town.

Just me and Ruby.

Alone.

Again.

I'm starting to become addicted to her.

Starting?

Ha.

Too late.

It's already happened.

CHAPTER NINETEEN

RUBY

The day you decide you like someone is weird. Like, I know all these things about this person. Good, bad, silly, whatever, and suddenly my brain is like, *well, I think we should see them naked and also let them see you naked.*

And then your heart races or your palms get sweaty when you see them. Suddenly, you're thinking of them the moment you wake up, throughout the day, and before you go to bed, constantly checking your phone to see if maybe, just maybe, they were thinking of you too.

What is the science behind this? How does this happen?

And how in the world did it happen with me and Declan?

As soon as my eyes open, my mind is a jumble of thoughts.

This trip has turned into one of the sexiest weekends I've ever had. I'll never forget the things we have done in the room, but also, last night was insane.

Somehow, Declan scored us a dinner at Hell's Kitchen. Normally, it has a six-month wait-list, but he called right after someone canceled, so we got lucky. Then he purchased tickets to the Cirque show right outside the restaurant.

It was the best spontaneous date I've ever had.

I mean, really, the only spontaneous date I've ever had.

We talked, we laughed, held hands, and kissed as if we were living a completely different life. It was us, but not us.

It's all so … confusing.

I didn't plan to want a boyfriend, and I know that a weekend of fun by no means is what we are, but I'm not stupid. I've developed feelings for this man, and I can't deny it.

I turn onto my side to admire the man lying next to me. His large body looks like everything he would do is rough and intense.

I smile. Alright, so there is a side of him like that, but the rest of this man is pure kindness, and I can't believe I resisted him for so long.

I missed out on getting to know the real him because I get so focused on other people's opinions.

I had a hunch that knowing Declan would result in making me fall for him, and I wasn't wrong.

He's everything I'd be looking for in a man.

But I guess it doesn't really matter, does it? Once we leave this room, we go back to who we were before we got here, because that was the deal we made two nights ago.

Well, minus the snarky comments from me.

I could never go back to that now that I know this side of him. The flirty side. The side that made me feel more confident in who I am than I have in years.

I close my eyes and roll to lay on my back.

This urge to snuggle against Declan right now, to hold his hand as we walk around this city again, across the airport, anywhere really, hits me in a rush.

It's not practical.

We are simply two people who are attracted to each other and randomly got stuck in a room together with one bed who also happen to live together back home.

The tension from always being near the other was thick, and we weren't strong enough to hold back.

It's as simple as that.

I groan and press the heels of my palms into my eyes.

How many more excuses am I going to come up with for why I made the choices I made?

I like Declan. I think a part of me always has.

"I sure hope you're groaning because our flight back to Lovers is today and that means we have to go back to our own beds tonight."

I let out a soft laugh.

I might be now.

"Nope."

I roll to my side, tucking my hands under the side of my face as I lie there and look at him. He rolls to his side, too, and studies me.

I smile, because when it comes to Declan Young these days, that's all my face wants to do.

I like the way he looks at me.

I don't want to like it.

The rush of emotions that comes with it is almost too much.

"Alright, what's wrong then?" he asks and props his head up to wait for my answer. His eyes stare so deeply into mine, it feels like he's trying to read my mind.

I shrug. "It's nothing."

"It's not nothing. You can talk to me, Ruby."

He reaches for my face, resting a hand on my cheek and leaning in to kiss me.

I let him, but then the worry sets in.

"You … you remember our deal, right?" I ask.

He pauses for another kiss and nods.

"Yep."

And then he pulls back, flipping the sheets off him and getting out of bed. He has boxers on, but they are tight and leave little to the imagination.

"Good. Because, um, we…"

Why is his body so pretty? I mean, I work out, too, but I don't have lines the way he does.

"If anyone is going to forget the deal we made, it's you because of the way you're looking at me."

I smirk.

"It's hard not to."

He sits on the bed as he pulls his shirt on. I sit up so that we can talk face-to-face. "You're still good to keep this all here, right?" he asks.

I nod quickly. That question alone is all I need to know that he's not overthinking this the way I am.

"Of course, yes."

"Good." He nods and then climbs back into the bed with me.

I knew the outcome, but that doesn't mean my heart doesn't sink a little at how easily he makes all this out to be.

He swoops an arm around me and jerks me to his chest.

I wrap my arm around him and then crawl into his lap to get the deepest hug that I can.

"We don't have to meet everyone downstairs for a couple of hours, so …" He draws the last word out, so I finish the sentence for him, my stomach growling on cue.

"So, we should order room service."

His laugh makes his whole body shake.

"That's exactly what I was thinking."

"I bet." I smile, giving him a quick kiss before I get out of bed for the menu and give myself room to breathe away from him, even if for a split second.

"I think I'm going to get the blueberry pancakes with whipped cream."

"Ask for extra," he says with a wink, and my insides melt.

Being near him when we get home is going to be more than a challenge.

I'm praying I can handle it.

But until then, I want as much of him as I can get.

———

A BELLY FULL of food and three orgasms later, we somehow manage to make it to the lobby before the rest of the group, so I let myself lean into Declan for just a few seconds more.

I glance at my watch. We are ten minutes early.

"Should we go to the little shop and get the kids matching shirts?" I ask.

"To go with the two-pound bag of M&Ms we bought for them, sure, why not?"

I give him a playful shove, and we head for the store.

He comes up behind me, brushing his hand to my lower back.

"I love that dress on you," he says. "Your eyes stand out when you wear it."

I glance down at the blue maxi dress I chose for traveling today.

"This dress?"

He nods.

"I wear this all the time, and you've never said a word about it."

"And have you bite my head off for admitting that I was looking at you, no thanks."

I let out a laugh and nod.

"You're probably right."

Suddenly, he grabs my hand and pulls me deeper into the store toward the back corner. He spins me, but stops when we are face-to-face and he can capture my lips with his own. His fingers slide around my waist and over my ass, squeezing it.

I love that he loves my butt.

I shouldn't, because apparently, he only loves my butt in Vegas.

"I'm going to miss this when we get back," he admits and rests his forehead on mine.

Then maybe I was wrong to suggest we leave it here.

Then he kisses me again.

There is a spark in his eye.

I open my mouth to suggest we be more, but again, he moves on as if it were that simple.

"Hey, do you think this means you'll finally tell me why you didn't like me for so long?"

"No," I say quickly and turn to find a shirt for Max.

He's quick to grab my hand and pull me back.

"Please," he begs, leaving it at just one word.

"You'll laugh. Even I am aware of how silly it was."

His grin widens, and I shake my head.

I want to be annoyed with him, but I can't. Everything is different now. Before I was snappy. Now... every part of me wants to flirt with him.

"Don't do that or I won't tell you."

His expression immediately turns serious.

"I'm ready."

"Okay," I blow out a breath. "In school, I was smart."

"Alright ..."

"But the teachers loved to remind me that although I was smart, I was never smarter than Declan Young. Even though we weren't even close in grade."

His brows dip in confusion, so I jump straight to a few examples, with voices to go with them.

"Wonderful scores, Ruby, you're right here in second place under Declan. So many votes on this one, but not as many as Declan Young. We almost have a school record with Ruby Asher, but she didn't quite beat—"

"I think I get it."

"But then," I say, and he groans.

"There's more?"

I nod.

"Then you moved back the same week as me and Max, and everyone in town just loved that you were back."

"Same for you though."

This time I shake my head. "I don't think so. Everyone praises your day-to-day life, Declan. It was annoying. Here I am, a single parent who shows up for her kid and who owns her own business, too, but they only see me as the girl who …"

My words trail off as I think of how to phrase it.

"The girl who what?" Declan grabs my hand and pulls me closer to him.

"The girl who got pregnant and left."

"No one thinks that, Ruby."

"They do."

"Well, fuck 'em. Who cares what they think?"

"Me. Apparently."

His gaze stays on mine for what feels like a lifetime.

Suddenly, I hear my brother's voice.

Declan and I break apart, and I grab the first shirt I see in Max's size.

I'd almost forgotten where we are and how this is supposed to be ending right here.

Just when it's my turn at the register, Declan steps in front of me with his things.

"Now, now, Ruby, have you not learned anything?"

I grin, not having a clue where he's going with this but eager to find out.

"I go first. Obviously."

When he turns to pay, I let out a giggle.

Of course, only Declan Young can take the reason I hated him for so long, turn it into a joke, and make me fall for him even more.

He winks when he's done paying and walks off.

I'm in so much trouble.

CHAPTER TWENTY

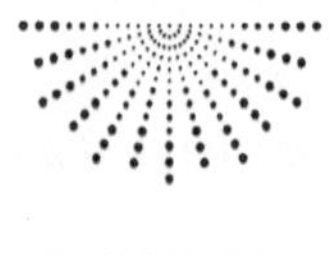

DECLAN

It's been a long, *long* three days.

Ever since Vegas, the energy between Ruby and I has been intensified.

It's a given when you do the things that we did together, but it goes past being attracted to one another.

Beyond the lust we have toward the other.

Beyond the way I'm forced to resist touching her when I want to. Especially when I catch her watching me. Which is just about as much as I watch her.

I crave Ruby Asher. I want to hold her in my arms the way I did those two nights. I want to wake up to her small laugh and the way her face lights up when she sees me next to her. I want to be the one standing in the bathroom brushing my teeth next to her and our eyes meeting in the mirror with a silent agreement that sleep will be non-existent for the night.

I want more.

So much more.

But the timing isn't right. She deserves someone who can give her 100 percent.

My fingers fly over the keyboard, finishing the end of an email to Steven. I need an update on *everything,* stat.

"Declan!" Max runs inside the back door, with Susie right behind him. "Is it time to go to the festival yet?"

I glance at my watch, fully knowing that Summer Fest has been in full swing for at least an hour now. Given this is Lovers, I'm sure the town started early.

They love a good festival and have them for the tourists. Almost every weekend during the summer

"I ..."

"Oh, Mom, good! Can we go now?"

Fuck.

Ruby has entered the room, and she looks gorgeous.

Short skintight black athletic shorts and a coral oversized shirt. Her hair is in a messy bun and her face is makeup free.

She looks like I need to sweep her into my arms, take her up to her room, and make sure she knows just how much I crave her.

I let out a sigh when our eyes meet.

Of course, Max breaks the trance. "Please, please."

He claps his hands and bounces his brows as if he just revealed a grand idea.

I chuckle, my eyes again finding Ruby's.

Should we? mine says to her.

Do you have to ask? I'm convinced she says back as she gives a slight nod.

"Let's go," I say and stand.

It's not that I try to avoid the festivals— it's just that they all start to blur together, so I'm picky about the ones I go to. Seems Ruby and I have that in common.

But the kids love every single one no matter the fact that they all look exactly the same. The one change is the name and the occasional game or two.

"Are we walking together?" I ask as we all move for the front door.

"No," Ruby quips.

My neck practically snaps as I look at her.

Is she mad at—oh.

She winks at me and walks out the door.

Susie and Max take the lead as we walk toward Main Street.

"How's your day?" I ask, bumping her arm with mine.

"Eww, Dec, are we really going to be those people? The ones who slept together and now they just create small talk."

I beam at her, soaking in the way she called me Dec. A lot of people call me that, but never Ruby.

I think she might be my favorite person to use my nickname.

If she doesn't want small talk, I'll just cut to the point of what I'm really thinking.

"You look sexy today."

"Dec!" she scolds and then smacks my arm. "No."

I chuckle again. "What do you want from me?"

"I don't know." She tosses her hands up. "Ask me about work or something."

"How's work?"

Her laughter catches me off guard.

"Good. Thank you for asking. I signed a new client today."

"That's wonderful. Tell me more."

She playfully shoves me and rolls her eyes. "Better, but you don't have to keep asking me about work."

"Why not? I genuinely want to know. I've seen your work, Ruby. You're good. More than good. The whole concept of your talent amazes me."

To that, she pauses, her gaze latching onto mine.

"You've checked out my work?"

I nod. "Is that not okay?"

"It's fine. I just … why?"

I shrug. "Why not?"

"Because you don't need graphic design work."

"Doesn't mean I can't still be interested in what you do. I actually recommended you to a friend who is rebranding his restaurant—"

"In Chicago?"

"Yeah." I smile. "Did he call you?"

She nods. "That's my new client."

"Good."

"So, I got him because of you?" Her smile starts to fall.

"No," I reply quickly. "I only told him to check out your website. You did the work, Ruby. Don't ever think otherwise."

"Mom!" Max calls out before Ruby can say a word.

She follows her son but glances over her shoulder twice before we reach Summer Fest.

We spot her brothers, the girls, and her father instantly. It's hard not to when Hudson has a booth outside his bar and Brooke has one outside her bakery, which are right next to one another.

Weaving through the crowd as we make our way over, I take in the music playing from the town speakers, the booths serving food, the people dancing in front of the dance studio, and a couple of the little boutique store owners who are outside with their best sellers on display. The street is lined with wooden picnic tables, and there isn't a free one in sight.

I'll give it to the town, for as much as I think these things are overkill, it sure does bring in good business for everyone.

Sheriff Sloan, Brooke's father, walks out of his daughter's bakery. He waves a quick greeting and is on his way to keep an eye on the town.

Not that much goes on here to keep track of.

"Brownies!" Susie cheers and then looks at me with pleading eyes. "Can I get one?"

"Go for it," I tell her and hand her some cash.

She and Max disappear into the bakery, running up to Luca and Miles standing in line and leaving Ruby and I on the sidewalk.

"Ruby, hi," a female voice says from behind us.

I turn at the same time as Ruby to see who it is.

I have no clue, but Ruby forces a smile.

"Clarissa, hey, I didn't know you were back in town."

"Just for the weekend." Clarissa's eyes drift from Ruby to me. "I don't believe we have met. I'm Clarissa," she says and holds out her hand.

"Declan Young."

Clarissa gasps. "*The* Declan Young?"

I do not like the way she said that.

"Maybe," I say.

"Wow, Ruby, from one millionaire to the next. I *love* your taste in men."

I glance between her and Ruby, looking for a sign, but I don't catch on.

Even then, I don't appreciate whatever this Clarissa is insinuating.

"You don't know what you're talking about," I practically growl at the woman, and she steps back. "I think you owe—"

Ruby's hand rests on my arm.

"Have a great weekend while you're here, Clarissa," she says and turns to walk off.

I follow instantly.

"Ruby," I call out. It's clear she's on a mission to get away from me, or Clarissa, as quickly as possible.

"She's wrong," Ruby turns to face me. "You defended me, and you don't even know the story, and I don't … I'm not … I don't care about the money."

Her lip starts to shake. I grab her hand and pull her away from the crowd. Since Hudson's Bar is at the end of the block, I round the corner there, stopping when she leans against the brick building.

I step closer to her and tilt her chin up so she'll look at me.

"What just happened?"

She bites her bottom lip and it drives me insane as I wait for her answer.

"Clarissa said I had a type, and I don't. I mean, I do, but it's not money."

"I never once thought you only liked me for my money, Ruby."

She nods, but I can see in her eyes that she's still not okay.

I don't ask anything more; I just stand there, holding her hand in mine until she's ready.

Finally, after a minute, she lets out a breath.

"I didn't really understand how much money the Davenports had when I got pregnant," she says quietly.

I keep my gaze locked on hers, grateful that she wants to open up to me, and she goes on.

"I just knew that leaving with them was going to open opportunities I couldn't get here. Opportunities that would be good for me as a young mom and help set me up for when I'm older and need to provide for Max. I didn't think the entire town would think I betrayed them and chose money over them."

I frown.

Ruby choosing to leave at seventeen to have a baby in a place she'd never been, surrounded by people she didn't know, all so she could give her kid the best life is a selfless choice that most adults wouldn't make.

If anyone thinks otherwise, they're idiots.

"No one thinks that."

She grunts. "You were there just now."

"Clarissa doesn't count. She doesn't live here. Only those

with real estate in their name here count. This town loves you and is lucky as hell to have you in it. I know they know it, too."

She twists her mouth, and the urge to bend down and kiss her hits me strongly. To feel her under my hands again. Her soft skin, plump lips, and to hear her moans as she comes over and over.

Her hand flattens against my chest, her fingers curling around my shirt. I lean closer, but then a horn honks nearby, breaking the trance.

As if I didn't need the reminder of why kissing Ruby again is a bad idea, my phone rings in my pocket.

The caller ID ruins my entire day.

Davenport Inc.

CHAPTER TWENTY-ONE

RUBY

It's officially been one week since we got home from Vegas, and I don't think I can keep this secret for much longer.

The tension at home is painful, and Declan and I keep finding ourselves in these little moments. His hand brushes my back while we pass each other in the kitchen or I look up from my work at the kitchen table to find him watching me. Or we are watching a movie with the kids and his arm finds its way to the back of the couch and his fingers play with my hair. Just being in the same room as him is tempting, and I swear—I swear—that despite how casually he left things in that hotel room, he's finding any reason to touch me.

Not to mention the way he compliments me on everything I do.

It's … he's … I don't know what to do anymore.

Do I tell him that I take it back? What if he doesn't agree because it's complicated? Do I just keep going how we are and pray neither of us snaps and ruins everything?

Which is why I have decided that keeping it bottled up is the wrong answer and, if I share my worries with the ones I trust the most, maybe I can get different perspectives and decide how to proceed.

Declan and Susie have only seven more weeks with us, and I don't want to ruin the rest of the summer by making the wrong choice.

Like always, I walk right into Brooke's house as if I own it.

I make a mimosa, grab a turkey and pesto sandwich Brooke made, and join the girls outside on the back patio.

Shay wasn't feeling well, so she stayed home.

Quinn is telling us why she will be gone for only two weeks on her next trip—apparently, that's the time limit on how long she and Miles can be separated.

It's cute.

I'm happy my brother found her.

I down my mimosa, stand to make another, then notice all eyes are on me.

"What?"

They exchange glances with each other, and Sadie smirks.

"Is everything okay?"

I nod. "Yes."

"Are you sure?"

I nod, but it quickly turns into a head shake. "I need advice."

I flop back into my seat, leaning my head onto the back of the couch, where I close my eyes.

"Declan and I had sex in Vegas, and we agreed to keep it there, but now I'm not so sure that's what I want. He seems to be fine with it, or at least, he's hiding it better than me."

"Wow," Sadie says. "This is huge."

"I know, and it's complicated for so many reasons, but I was so wrong about him, you guys. I hate that I disliked him for so long."

"Aww," Grace says and then rests her chin in her hands. "So, what now?"

"That's what I need advice for. I don't know how to go about this. I'm sure he has his reasons for why this couldn't go on, but I don't know what they are. We just agreed."

"Then I say that's where you start." Brooke nods. "What are your reasons?"

"The kids for one, and ..."

"And ..." Quinn encourages me.

"I don't want people to think that I only like men who have money."

All of them erupt into laughter.

"Who cares what people think?" Sadie asks. "If he makes you happy, I think you need to talk to him."

She makes it sound so easy.

I wish I didn't care so much what other people think of me, but I spent so long trying to impress Colt's parents that somewhere along the way, it's now a part of me.

I don't want it to be part of me.

No one can fix that but me.

"I think you should go for it." Brooke grins.

Sadie nods. "Me too."

"Same."

"Agreed."

"If he were just some guy you had a crush on, you wouldn't come looking for advice. But this is Declan. That man had eyes for you the first time I saw you two in a room together."

"No, he didn't," I say and can feel my cheeks warm from blushing.

"Yes, he did."

I try to hide the smile on my face.

"He's a really good dad, and he's kind and thoughtful. Living with him has been much easier than I thought, and I get excited that he's there. It makes me sad to think they will move out eventually. I like having him near me."

"And you trust him?" Quinn asks.

Her question takes me by surprise, but not for the reason you'd think. It surprises me because I don't have to think twice when I say, "Yes, I do."

Sadie squeals with a clap.

Quinn's phone rings, interrupting the conversation, but that's okay.

I know what I need to do.

I need to forget what everyone is saying or thinking about me and focus on me and Declan only. Who I want to be and who I think we could be.

It's easier said than done, but there's only one way to give it a chance.

———

AN UNFAMILIAR CAR is parked outside the house when I get home a couple of hours later.

I pull into the garage then head inside; the noise of two kids laughing hits me the moment I open the door.

All eyes shift to me

"You must be Ruby!" An older woman with gray hair cut into a bob rushes toward me.

An older man sitting next to Declan on the couch chuckles.

"Now, dear, don't overwhelm her. This is her house, and she didn't know we were coming."

"They just showed up maybe ten minutes ago," Declan adds.

"Declan's mom and dad brought cookies!" Max says between bites.

"And presents!" Susie adds, pointing to a couple of new games on the table.

Declan's mother wraps me in a hug and holds tight. "I'm just so happy to finally meet you in person. I've heard so much about you."

I shift my gaze to Declan, who has his head down, shaking it back and forth.

"Not that much, Mom."

"A little from you but mostly from Susie."

His mother pulls back and holds me at the shoulders. "You truly are an amazing woman, and this little girl looks up to you. Not to mention you helping my son out when he needed it. I'm not so sure there is anything a mother can do to repay you."

She turns and grabs the cookie tray. "I baked these for you."

"Oh, that's not necessary," I say as Declan's dad stands.

"I'm Troy, and this is my wife, Emma."

"Oh gosh, where are my manners? I never even told you my name. I'm so nervous," Emma looks over her shoulder at Declan. "She's so gorgeous. You forgot to mention that. Lord knows, you have two good eyes and can see it."

Declan rolls those good eyes and grins.

I break out into a laugh as Troy shakes my hand.

For a brief moment, I'd feared meeting Declan's parents, thinking they would be too similar to the last ones I met, but I was wrong. So incredibly wrong.

"Would you two like to stay for dinner?" I ask, not just because it's the polite thing to do but because getting to know them is something I very much want right now.

"Oh, we don't want to intrude."

"You're not," I rush out when I see Declan beginning to reply. "Let me whip up something real quick."

"I'll help," Emma says, and we head for the kitchen, both kids right behind us.

Troy excuses himself to use the restroom.

I take this moment to move closer to the man I've been falling for.

He stands as I approach and leans in close.

"Are you sure this is okay? They just showed up. Said they wanted to see me since they barely saw me before Vegas."

"It's more than okay." I rub my hand down his arm.

His gaze drifts to where we touch and then flickers to mine.

Our fingers touch and he doesn't pull away. I lace our fingers together.

The smile he gives me is like an electric current to my heart, which begins to race.

"Where are you—" Emma's voice startles us, and I pull my hand away from his.

"Oh, I'm so sorry. Carry on." His mother steps into the living room and then smiles as she walks out.

We both laugh, and Declan is right behind me as we head toward the kitchen, his hand on my lower back the entire way.

Now isn't the right time to tell him about the choices I made while I was with the girls, but this moment right here tells me that maybe I'm not alone in my thoughts.

CHAPTER TWENTY-TWO

DECLAN

I can't sleep.

I flip the covers off me and grab my computer. I prop myself against the headboard. Might as well check my emails.

I click on one, scan it, then I click on the next and scan that one, too.

Yet, if someone were to walk in here right now and ask me what I just read, I wouldn't have an answer.

My mind is 100 percent focused on Ruby.

This past week has been torture. I'd hyped myself up all day to talk to her. To tell her that maybe we made a mistake by agreeing to end this in Vegas, but then my mind kept going back to whether or not I could be who she needs, who my company needs, and who my daughter needs all at the same time.

The point of being with someone is to have a partner, right? That person you grow with and who is there for you through the good and the bad. We could be that person for each other, couldn't we?

Watching her with my parents tonight was a sight I never planned to see anytime soon, but something about the way my mom fawned over her and how Ruby laughed at my dad's horrible jokes … everything just fits.

I've never felt so content before.

It kills me that she's right upstairs. That in under sixty seconds I could be up there with her. I would have to be quiet, sure, but she's *right there*.

I shove my laptop aside and grab my phone, opening up my text thread with Ruby.

DECLAN:

Are you awake?

The dots appear almost instantly, as if she'd been waiting for me to message her.

RUBY:

Yes. I can't sleep.

DECLAN:

Neither can I.

RUBY:

Why not?

I debate whether I should tell her the truth. I don't want to scare her away. But I'm not about to start whatever this is with a lie.

DECLAN:

I'm thinking about sneaking up there to see you.

The dots appear and then go away.

Then they appear again and her text is almost instant.

RUBY:

Okay.

That's all the assurance I need to sneak out of my room.

A couple of the steps creak, but I pause long enough to be sure they don't wake Susie.

I tiptoe across the middle floor and to the stairs that lead to Ruby's room. Her door is closed, but it's clear that she still has her light on.

I find her wearing a mismatched pair of pajama shorts and a t-shirt, sitting up in her bed with her computer the way I was.

"Hi," She whispers.

"Hi," I whisper back.

She closes her computer and puts it aside, then she meets me at the foot of her bed. She reaches out to touch my chest, her hands sliding up to my neck, and my head pounds louder than ever before.

But when her gaze locks onto mine, I know without words that her mind is in the same place as mine.

"How did we ever think we could keep this to just two nights?" I ask her, snaking my hand around her body to pull her against me.

God, it feels good to have her in my arms again.

She lets out a small laugh.

"I have no idea."

She pushes to her feet and presses her lips to mine.

Fuck. I missed her.

When she pulls back, her smile fades.

"What if it doesn't work out and the kids suffer from it?"

"That won't happen, but I can promise you that I won't let us impact their friendship."

"What if this affects your friendship with my brothers?"

"Your brothers are great, Ruby, but for you, I'd risk it."

"What if I can't get past the things people say about us and I freak out?"

"Then we work through it, together."

Her mouth twists.

"Look, Ruby, I'm not going to beg you to be with me, but let me be very clear. I like you. A lot. If this isn't something you think you'll ever be ready for, I need you to tell it to me straight."

The room fills with silence.

Her eyes latch onto mine as her breathing picks up.

Instead of using words, she launches herself at me. I catch her in time to help wrap her legs around my hips.

Her lips meet mine, and she kisses me desperately.

She tilts her head to deepen the kiss, sliding her tongue into my mouth to dance with my own.

"I don't want to tell the kids or anyone yet. Let's do this for us right now and figure out the rest later."

"I can do that," I tell her and take a seat on her bed, letting her straddle me.

We don't break apart except to pull our shirts over our heads.

I grip her breast and give it a small squeeze.

She moans at my touch; my cock twitches beneath her.

I scoot back and then flip us over to lay her on her back.

I unbutton her shorts and slowly slide them down her legs, taking her panties with them.

Once she's bared to me, I settle my face between her legs, licking and sucking her glistening center until she's pulling on my hair and coming on my tongue.

She moans my name in a whisper, and I reach for her nightstand.

"What are you doing?" she asks.

I wink.

"You don't think I forgot about your friends here, did you?"

Her cheeks turn red.

"Don't get shy on me now."

I grab both of them and hold them up for her to pick one.

Yeah, I'd love to use them at the same time, but I plan to have her come the second time on my own cock, so I don't want to get carried away.

She points to the purple one.

As I put the other one back, I spot the gel she must use with them.

"Ruby, I'll never be the same knowing this drawer is up here next to you each night."

She grins wickedly. "Then I probably shouldn't tell you that I've thought of you while using them."

"Fuck, really?"

She nods.

"That's hot."

I grab the gel, and even though we don't need it, I squirt a small bit right between her legs, then I reach forward and massage it into her pussy, sliding two fingers inside of her.

Her back bows off the bed, and she grips the sheets.

I could watch her like this all fucking day.

I press the tip of the vibrator against her and flip the switch on.

"Shit."

My cock gets harder as I push the toy inside of her. The vibrations against my hand are intense. I can't imagine what it's like inside of her.

So, I slide a finger inside with it to feel it.

"Oh!" She lets out a breath.

"Breathe, Ruby, you've got this, but don't forget to be quiet."

I push the dildo in a little more and watch as her breathing becomes erratic. Keeping it inside of her, I reach down to remove my sweats and pull out my dick.

I stroke it twice and then I shift my body up to rub my tip against her clit.

I groan the moment I feel the vibrator pulsing against my own cock.

I rub myself against her faster, now moving the dildo in and out.

"Declan, I'm … I'm …"

I pull the vibrator all the way out, flip her to her stomach and pull her up by her hips. I keep her legs pinned together and straddle them before lining myself up with her entrance and pushing in.

"Oh my God!" she cries into the sheets as I slam into her once, twice, and then a third time before her pussy grips my cock and I come with her.

I pump until the last bit of my orgasm is gone, and then I roll off her and let her breathe.

I might have gotten a little carried away.

I rub her back, waiting for her to look at me.

When she does, she's grinning and starts to laugh.

"Let's do that again," she says.

I lean forward and press my lips to hers.

I know without a doubt that whatever Ruby Asher is willing to give me, I'm going to take.

Even if I have to sneak up to her room every night for the rest of the summer.

CHAPTER TWENTY-THREE

RUBY

For the first time in as long as I can remember, we didn't have Sunday breakfast. Instead, we spent the morning and afternoon at the lake, opting to have Sunday dinner.

It's been a nice switch-up, but I'll be honest, after a day in the sun, all I want to do is shower, then snuggle up with a movie and Declan.

It's been three weeks of us stealing kisses here or there in the house. The kids are always around. I'm impressed with the restraint we've had during the day, because at night, we don't hold back.

I bite my lips to hide a smile. Just thinking about how, in a couple of hours, I'll get to be in his arms makes me giddy.

I want to laugh at how worried I'd been over being with him. He's been nothing but incredible, and even though it's only been a couple of months since this whole thing started, I feel like I know him better than I know anyone else.

Declan was bound to be a part of my life, I just didn't know how.

"Everything is coming along great and we're still on

schedule for you guys to move into the house in four weeks," Luca says to Declan.

"Great. I do have a few changes I'd like to make, but I'll stop by in the morning to go over those. Nothing major."

"Good." Luca chuckles. "It's a little late to change most of it."

"They're just additions to what we have going and some new ideas for the landscaping in the backyard."

I ignore the pit in my stomach at the mention of him moving out.

I knew this was part of the plan, but after our time together, I'm clearly feeling different about it.

At the same time, this thing with us has moved quickly, and it might be good for us to get space. I don't want to stop what we are doing, but it has gone at a pace I don't think is normal. Even if I do feel like everything about it is right.

Declan's eyes meet mine, and he smiles.

I look away quickly before anyone can see how I feel about him. The girls know, of course. It was hard not to have them in the loop after I asked for advice, but I know for a fact that none of them have told my brothers.

How do I know this? None of them have yet to punch Declan in the face—or well, mention it to me.

I take the long route to the house, pausing to check on one of my flowerpots as I round the table so I can walk behind Declan's chair and run my hand across his shoulders.

It's reckless. I just can't seem to keep my hands to myself anymore.

I take another step, but Declan's voice stops me.

"Hey, babe, will you grab me another beer when you go in?" he asks from across the patio.

"Yep," I say, as I'm already heading into the house.

I take one more step, then pause. I'm staring straight ahead at nothing, but silence fills the backyard, and I sense every set of eyes on me as I reach for the door handle.

Shit.

Shit.

Did he … and then I …

I should drop my hand from the handle and go back to what I was doing, but I've already responded, so no matter what choice I make from here, there will be an interrogation. I'm part of the Asher family, and all of them are watching me.

I clear my throat, hold my head high, and open the door without looking back at anyone. I move for the fridge, running through the questions they'll ask.

Why did he call you babe?

Why did you respond?

No, why did you respond so naturally?

Why does it sound like he calls you that often?

Are you two dating?

Suddenly, the sliding door opens, startling me from my thoughts.

"What are you doing?" I ask as Declan rushes toward me.

"Checking on you." He rubs the back of his neck. "That sort of just slipped out. I couldn't handle the silence out there, and I didn't want to say anything without talking to you first. However we handle this is entirely up to you."

He's so freaking adorable and sweet, and his sexiness only increases when he says things like that.

This is entirely up to you.

It's my choice.

"I …I'm not sure."

"And that's perfectly fine. If you're not ready to say anything, we won't."

He slides a hand around my waist and tugs me toward him, placing the sweetest kiss on my lips.

"And you're okay with that?" It's almost a whisper.

"Baby, all I need is you. So, if you don't want to tell them, I'll be fine." He kisses me again.

"But you want them to know?"

"The day you give me the go-ahead, I'm going to make sure everyone knows that I'm yours."

It's been so nice living in this bubble where no one knows about us. We get to just be us with no outside opinions, but eventually people will find out.

I've fallen so hard for this guy, I don't know why I should keep it in anymore. I can handle the comments. I know I can.

Falling in love is wild.

One minute you know you really like this guy and you want to hang out with him and kiss him and more, then all of a sudden, something clicks and you know without a doubt that this right here, the way he's holding you, is the way you want to be held for the rest of your life.

"I want to tell them," I say. That's all I manage to get out before he jerks back, eyes wide and his smile even wider.

"Really?"

I nod. "Really."

He rubs the back of his neck and then looks to the back door. Still ginning like a kid on his birthday. "Okay. Yay."

In an instant, he's wrapping both arms around me and spinning me in the kitchen. My laughter is unstoppable.

"Did you just say yay?" I ask, grinning as he sets me on my feet.

"I did."

I giggle more.

"It's a yay moment. I'm one decision away from thrusting my arm into the air and dancing."

"All because I want to tell people?"

"Yes. I would have kept us a secret for my whole life if it

meant I got to have you in it, Ruby, but now that I know I get to live openly with you, fuck, it feels good."

He kisses me again and then steps back.

"Okay, how do we do this? Just walk out there? What if Miles hits me? I feel like he might. Luca will feel my yay vibes, and Hudson will be fine with it and your—"

"You've really thought about this, haven't you?"

"Baby, you come with a big family. A family who loves you very much, and I care what they think, yes."

He blows out a breath.

"Let's do this."

I lace my fingers with his.

A sliver of guilt washes over me at what he's clearly been battling, but then my heart swoons. He had said he would respect and support every choice I make.

He kept his word.

He slides the back door open, and we step out hand in hand.

No one is looking at us, so Declan clears his throat and places his arm over my shoulders.

Luca looks up, grins, and then goes back to eating.

"That's it?" I ask, almost disappointed that none of them are acting the way I assumed they would.

"We would have had more of a reaction if the kitchen window hadn't been open that entire time," Hudson says with a smirk. Then he winks at me while pointing his fork at Declan. "Hurt her and I'm not afraid to punch you in the face."

"I'll be right after him," Miles says, glancing between us and letting out a sigh. "Or first, as you mentioned."

"I'd hear you out, then probably punch you on account of the fact she is my sister" is Luca's answer. "Also, you're welcome."

"You're welcome?" I repeat. "For what?"

"For so many things. Not being able to move up the date on his house, putting the idea of living with you in his head at basketball, and mostly for putting you in the same room in Vegas."

"You planned that?" I ask, shocked.

"Well, not really,"—he grins—"but I'm not mad they happened. Fate and all that."

"Fate and all that." Declan chuckles. "What if she still hated me? Then what would you say?"

Luca shrugs. "I tried."

The table erupts into laughter.

"For the record, I was into Ruby the moment she walked out that door last summer after Susie put a hole in the fence."

"What?" I lean back to look at him. "Really?"

"Yeah, you walked out, and like a lovesick fool, I swear my heart skipped a beat. But then you found out who I was and basically declared war, so I never did anything about it. I had no idea our kids would become best friends and that I'd spend the next year getting to know you."

"But I was mean to you."

"And I was oddly into it."

I gape at him. He's never told me this.

"I can see your wheels turning. I thought you were hot and you were fun to be around, even if you were snappy."

I shake my head, but can't stop the smile from forming on my lips.

"You sure are something."

He shrugs.

"I'm whatever you need me to be, baby."

"Oh no. I'll stop you right there. None of that." Miles groans.

I point a finger at my brothers. "I sat here and watched all of you love your ladies this last year. Deal with it."

"Here, here," my dad says and holds up his water.

"Dad, what?" Hudson says with a laugh, and the others join in.

When their conversation falls back to Hudson's upcoming hockey season, I glance up to Declan.

"That wasn't so bad."

"No, it wasn't, but I'm sure glad it's over."

"Why? Scared?"

"No, because now I can do this anytime I want."

He hooks an arm around me and kisses me right there in front of everyone.

"Told ya!" Max says, and Declan and I pull apart to look at him and Susie.

Susie is grinning like a kid at Christmas, while Max rolls his eyes.

They quickly go back to playing, and we all continue as if I didn't just make an announcement that changed my life in a huge way.

I move to lean into Declan again, but his phone rings. He pulls it out, and a scowl forms on his face.

"I need to take this," he says, placing a quick kiss on the top of my head and then walks back into the house.

I watch him as he leaves, completely unaware that I won't see him again for almost three hours.

Or that for the next couple of weeks, he'll work more than he has all summer.

CHAPTER TWENTY-FOUR

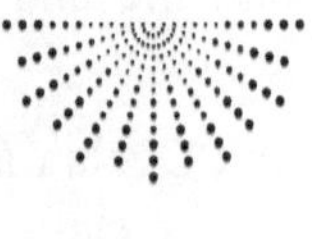

DECLAN

I pull up in front of the house Luca is building for me, and Ruby barely waits for me to park before she's unbuckling and getting out.

It wouldn't be crazy to think that she's more excited than I am.

The smile on her face should put me at ease.

I want her to move in with us. She and Max.

I want more with her. Them.

Now that the entire town has known for the past two weeks, there is no hiding the fact that I fell hard for this woman.

I wouldn't have it any other way.

"It's almost ready?" she asks, rubbing her hands together.

I nod.

"Can you give me a tour, or will Luca freak?"

I chuckle at the mischief in her eyes over the idea of her brother losing his mind.

"It's my house. I can do anything I want with it. Let's take a tour."

We both head for the front door. With her hand in mine, I unlock it.

There is a lot left to do, but it's still on schedule for the deadline.

"Wow, I love how open the floor plan is on this level," she says and sighs.

"Me too. I wanted as much light as possible in this space, where Susie would want to bring her friends. I want to be *that* house. The hangout house."

Ruby grins.

"So do I."

Our eyes meet.

"That's good to know."

"Mm-hmm."

I grab her hand and pull her down the hall to the right. "This is where Susie's room will be, then the guest room, and another spare room. There is a bathroom attached to each one for privacy."

"I love that."

I pull her back down the hall and across the open room to the hallway on the other side.

"Here is the office and bathroom for this floor."

"Oh wow, this room is huge. You could get two, maybe even three desks in here. Which is good, considering how much you've been working lately."

I know she doesn't mean for her comment to hurt, but it does. I've been so head down trying to get this purchase done before Davenport Inc., that I haven't given Ruby as much time as I should.

I'm slipping, and I hate it.

"Come see upstairs," I say, not commenting on her remark.

"Do you have a lot of rooms up here?" she asks as we ascend the stairs.

"Just one."

We reach the top, where there is a small platform that I plan to have a reading chair and some built-in shelves. Then we step through a double doorframe into the master bedroom.

She gasps.

"Declan, this is going to be … wow. I cannot think of another word right now."

Standing in the middle of the room, you can see where the bathroom is being placed to the left and the large walk-in closet next to it. On the right, it has floor-to-ceiling windows with a balcony that looks out over the lake.

"This is the perfect place for a slow morning with some coffee and a book or my computer to work on some designs," she says, walking up to the window. "This view would calm anyone."

I step up behind her, my hand brushing against her lower back and slinking around her hip to pull her toward me. She twists in my arms and rests her palms flat on my chest.

"What would you say if I told you that you could have that?"

"Here?" Her eyes go wide.

"Yes."

"In the mornings, I sleep over?"

"Or," I say with a nervous grin, "because you live here."

She steps back, her chest rising and falling on quick breaths.

"You … you want me to move in with you?"

"Yes, and Max, obviously. We already live together now, and if you haven't figured it out yet, Ruby Asher, I'm obsessed with you."

She laughs.

"It's a little obvious."

I chuckle and then press my lips to hers.

"Well?"

"Well … even though I can guess his answer, I need to talk to Max first."

"I would expect nothing less."

Our next kiss lasts only a second before she pulls back.

"You're sure about this?"

"Completely."

"This is a big decision. Are you ready for it?"

"More than anything. Are you?"

She nods instantly, and her fingers thread through my hair as she slips her tongue into my mouth.

She tastes like wintergreen and sugar, and I can't get enough.

I spin us and press her to the wall, my hand sliding over her curves and down her leg to tug her thigh up to my side.

When she hooks her heel to my lower back, I bunch her skirt up the lifted leg and touch my way to her inner thigh.

"Dec, what if my brother shows up?"

"He won't." I capture her mouth with mine and slide my fingers closer to her core.

"But what if he does?"

"Then I hope we hear him open the door. This place is empty and it echoes. We'll hear him."

"Okay," she says, then she's kissing me again and tilting her hips to give my hand better access.

At the start of the summer, she would have argued to no end, but that one simple word makes my heart swell. She trusts me, and she doesn't give trust easily.

I break the kiss and press my lips down her neck. Then I tug her panties to the side and slip my finger in.

"Oh," she breathes.

"That's all I get?" I tease and slip another finger in. "How about now?"

"Yeah, that's good."

"Good?"

She nods.

"You deserve better than good." I slide my other hand into my sweats, pulling them down far enough to release myself.

Stroking myself, I remove my fingers from her pussy and then rip her underwear off, instantly placing the head of my cock at her entrance to tease her.

"Shit," she hums when I press in just an inch.

"Is that still just *good* for you?"

"No … it's …"

I push in another inch.

"It's …

Another inch.

"If you can't form a sentence, then I'm doing it right."

I slam into her, and she screams out.

"Yes!"

"Play with yourself," I command, and she reaches between us without a second thought.

"I can't, this position won't let—"

I pull out, flip her around and hike her skirt up to show me her ass. Palm flat to her back, I force her to bend over slightly.

When I'm lined up, I push in.

"Fuck." Her hand slaps the wall. "Yes."

"You're so tight, baby. I love the way you feel around me. Now, do as I say and play with yourself. I want to feel you come around me, and I don't want to wait."

She runs a finger over my cock when she reaches down, and I nearly come undone.

I speed up, fucking her against the wall, the sounds of our breathing echoing through the house.

Our house.

This will be our house.

"Shit, Declan, I'm coming," she says, groaning.

I replace her hand with mine, circling her clit and drawing

out her orgasm, mine following right behind her and making me black out.

I pump my hips slowly to ride it out, but after the bliss fades and I've fixed myself back into my joggers and readjusted her skirt, I hold her still.

I kiss the back of her head, then her shoulders, and wrap my arms around her.

"I want to stay like this forever. I never knew I could feel at such peace."

"Yeah, standing here together?" she asks softly.

"No. When I'm holding you in my arms."

She turns and kisses my cheek.

"This is my favorite place to be, too."

————

THE AFTERNOON GETS AWAY from us, so by the time night falls, I'm sitting in Ruby's bed with my laptop while she sleeps next to me. Once the kids knew about us, they begged us to move rooms around and now both kids are in the basement and Ruby and I share her room. She's on her side facing away from me, one leg peeking out from the sheets, her hair splayed across the pillows.

She didn't bother getting dressed after we fooled around again tonight.

It's hard not to stare at her right now.

I'm not a sappy man, but fuck, this woman. I never thought I'd find this with anyone.

Luck was on my side, and I've never been so happy.

God damn, I'm feeling extra cheesy right now.

I open my email and my happiness fades when I see multiple emails from Steven with a red exclamation point in the subject line.

They all say that we need to talk. That it's urgent.

I grab my phone, noting there was a missed call from him this afternoon.

I shoot him a quick text to see if he's still awake.

No sooner than the message says delivered, my phone rings.

"One sec," I answer in a whisper.

"I'm sorry to call so late," Steven says.

I climb out of bed and sneak down the hall.

I wait for him to go on, but he doesn't.

The silence almost speaks louder than whatever it is that he needs to tell me.

My heart races and my stomach turns as if I'm going to be sick.

"What happened?"

I hear him let out a long breath. "TurnBlue Inc. gave notice to cancel their contract with us."

"Why?"

"We … missed a couple of deadlines that were required for them."

Silence fills the line.

"Declan, if we lose our biggest client, there's no way we can acquire Collins Corp."

The chills that cover my skin sting.

My back hits the wall as I slide down to sit.

The rest of this call requires it.

"I thought you said you could handle this."

"I thought I did."

"If they are giving notice, Steven, something has been going on that you haven't been telling me."

"I-I've done my best, but you working remotely has changed too much here. So unless we want to lose them and possibly more clients, we need you back here in the office."

He lets a moment pass before he adds.

"And not just for the weekend. We need you here. Permanently. Things aren't as smooth without you here."

My heart thuds louder and louder as I stare at the wall in front of me.

"Declan, did you hear me?"

"I heard you," I whisper. "We'll talk tomorrow."

I hang up, but I don't move.

My head drops forward and I close my eyes.

I hear sheets ruffling. Ruby. The woman who has changed my entire world in a matter of months.

The woman I can't imagine living life without.

What am I supposed to do now? Ask her to change her entire life for me? Ask her to move to a completely different town where I'll neglect her while I put time in at the office. Because let's face it, things are fucked, and I'll have to put in more time than I do now.

And she deserves better. She always has.

I clear my throat, but remain on the floor.

My heart breaks at the choice I have to make.

For me.

For her.

For all the people who trusted me to employ them and who depend on me to pay their bills and take care of their families.

For my company. The company that has given me and Susie everything we have but has taken so much from her, too.

But Ruby …

Ruby …

My Ruby.

I'm so fucking in love with her that it hurts.

My chest physically aches. I want to spend every moment of every day with her.

I want to marry her and have more kids with her and just *be with her.*

But what I want to do and what I need to do just might kill me.

CHAPTER TWENTY-FIVE

RUBY

Declan has been quiet all day.

I'm sure it's over what he asked me yesterday.

Living together is huge.

Living together was just supposed to be temporary and there was an end date.

What he's asking me doesn't come with an end date.

Or at least I hope it doesn't.

Is he already regretting asking me?

Was it an in-the-moment question?

I glance out the kitchen window to where he's sitting with Hudson. Hudson is talking away, using his arms, and Dec is just nodding.

Now, I know he isn't the kind of guy to chat your ear off, but he usually gives more to a conversation than a head nod.

We had invited my brothers and the girls over for pizza spontaneously—maybe having a full house isn't what he wanted today.

"What are we looking at?" Shay asks.

"Oh, crap." My hand goes to my chest. "You scared me."

She smiles.

"Are you standing here just admiring your man? You know, now that it's been a couple of weeks since everyone found out, you can finally go out without sneaking around?"

Her eyes start to well with tears.

This surely isn't something to cry about.

"I miss sneaking around. It was so much fun, and it was hot, too," she says and then looks to her left, then her right. "Is anyone upstairs?"

I laugh and then try to find something to keep myself busy.

"No, and you're not taking my brother up there."

"Dang it. Was I that obvious?"

"And more," I laugh.

She smiles. "Seriously though, that wrinkle between your eyes was in full force."

"I don't have a wrinkle."

"All of you Ashers have it." She shrugs. "Spill."

I cover my forehead with my hand.

"Yesterday Declan asked me to move in with him when his house is finished, but today, he's … off."

"Off how?"

"It's just a feeling I get. He's not been as touchy-feely."

Declan chooses this exact moment to walk into the house.

He freezes.

"Is everything okay in here?"

I nod.

Shay copies me.

Dec smirks and then kisses my forehead, rubbing my shoulder as he passes me to head down the hallway.

"That didn't seem off," Shay whispers.

My gaze follows his backside as he disappears up the stairs.

"No. I guess not," I say, but a weird feeling still nags at my stomach. Like the moment you know you're about to be sick.

I give Shay my best smile though.

There is no need for us to both worry when it's probably nothing.

"Good. Now, come hang out with us."

I follow, but my mind is still in the house with Declan.

"Hey, did you tell him you'd move in?" she asks as if it's an afterthought.

"Not yet."

She pauses to open the sliding door.

"Well, I bet that's your answer. You haven't given him one, so now he's all nervous."

"You think?"

That's not a completely unreasonable suggestion for his behavior.

"Yes. It has to be it."

Her words set me at an ease I didn't know I was missing.

I'll tell him tonight after the kids go to bed and it's just us.

Then I'll show him how every single night is going to be.

I make my way out to the table and take my seat.

My phone is sitting by my plate, and I happen to glance down at it at the same time a text comes through.

My entire body freezes when I see the name.

Barton Davenport.

Colter's dad is texting me?

With a shaky hand, I pick up my phone and open it.

BARTON DAVENPORT:

Call me. I have a deal you'll want to hear to erase the debt you have with me.

Phone in hand, I retreat to the house quickly to get this over with. I know that man well enough to know his persistence until he gets what he wants.

Closing my bedroom door, I start the call.

"I knew the mention of money would make you call me," he greets me.

"It's the mention of being done with you that spiked my interest," I say and my eyes go wide.

I've never spoken to him like that.

He chuckles, and it makes me cringe.

"Where was that fire when you were with my son?"

"What's the deal, Barton?"

"Also cutting to the chase. I like that too."

I wait in silence for him to go on.

"Your new boyfriend is getting in the way of my next business move. Convince him to back off, and I will consider all the debt you owe me as clear."

"I can't do that," I tell him without a second thought.

"Okay, then I retract my comment to not charge you interest. I will include interest on back payments as well."

"You can't do that."

"Oh, dear, I can do anything I want."

"I ..."

Saving that money would be huge for me. Just about as huge as if he were to start adding interest.

Shit.

"I'll sweeten the deal for you, Ruby. Get him to back down and I'll not only forgive your debt, but I will be sure that your design company is the required one for all my companies and my colleagues' extended companies. You'll never have to worry about money again. All you have to do is convince Declan to remove Young Technologies from this deal."

CHAPTER TWENTY-SIX

DECLAN

I'm going to be sick.

The kids fell asleep about half an hour ago, and I've been dragging my feet to get to bed. If I don't tell her now and she finds out I waited more than a day to tell her, I'll only make things worse.

I pause at the bottom of the steps. The kitchen has been scrubbed clean, the dusting done, and the dishes put away. There isn't anything else for me to do to put this off.

I'm avoiding the look in her eyes.

I'm avoiding the tears I know will come.

The fight she's going to give me.

I'm avoiding heartbreak for both of us. Because that's what it'll be.

I'm going to ask her to come with me, but I already know her answer.

But I have to ask. I'd never forgive myself if I didn't.

I take the steps slowly.

You love her.

She loves you.

You'll make it work.

She values communication, and that's exactly what I'm doing. I'm not keeping things from her, so it will all work out.

"Finally," her voice coos as I step into the room.

Ruby is lying on the bed in nothing but one of my shirts. She's on her side, with the hem lifted just enough to show that she isn't wearing anything underneath.

I swallow the dry lump in my throat.

"Come over here so I can tell you something." Her smile is like a punch to the gut.

Whatever she's going to tell me, I need to be sure I go first.

"So, I talked to Max about what you asked—"

"I need to move back to Chicago," I say quietly, cutting her off.

That wasn't how I planned for it to come out, but stalling didn't feel right either.

"What?" Her voice is even quieter.

She pulls my shirt down over her body and slowly stands in front of me.

"My biggest client is … it's complicated, and I've been working my ass off to close this deal. It's become one big mess, and both of those things require me to be in Chicago full-time right now."

She doesn't say anything, so I go on.

"I need to finish this deal. I have to."

"Why?"

"Because I do."

"I need to know why, Declan. You have to explain to me, or I can't—"

"Because it's why Susie's mom left," I cut her off. "She left because I put more work into my company than I did for her, and she didn't like that. She left Susie because of *me,* Ruby, and if we don't close this deal, then Susie will have lost her mom for nothing. I don't know if I can move on from the past if I don't."

I drop to sit on the bed. I've never said that aloud before. "Part of me thought if I never told anyone, it wasn't true. But it is."

Ruby quickly comes to sit next to me, and she hugs me tight.

My heart sinks. This company has cost me so much already, and it's about to cost me even more.

Ruby hand glides up and down my spine.

"I want you to stay here," she admits. "Because I'm selfish and I don't want to go a day without you."

"I know. I want to stay, too. Maybe I will—"

"But you have to go, Declan."

"What?" The tears in her eyes break me even more.

"You have to finish what you started. Not for Susie or me or anyone else—you have to do it for you. You'll either regret it or always wonder, and I won't be the reason for that."

"Then come with me," I say, cupping her face in my hands. "You and Max."

"I can't." She breaks into a sob. "If I'm going to move on from the past, too, I can't repeat it."

I hold her through the tears. One slips from my eyes, but I swipe it before she can see it.

"I'm not leaving you forever. We can make this work until I figure things out."

"No."

My entire body rears back as if she slapped me.

"What?"

"I won't do long distance."

I shake my head. "Why not? This isn't forever, I just need to go back and get a plan in place."

She holds her head high and takes a deep breath.

"So when will you be back? And then when will your job take you away from me again? How many times will it happen?"

She's right to ask me this.

"I don't know."

"And that's why I won't do it. It will only increase how much it hurts when we finally realize that one of us has to give up how far we've come. I won't do that to myself or you, and I absolutely will not do that to Max or Susie."

Shit.

"Ruby." I reach for her, but she steps back. "I lo—"

"Don't." She sniffles. "Please don't say it right now."

I let my hand fall between us.

She's right.

"When do you leave?" she asks.

"In two days."

She wipes her tears away and nods.

"I think you should sleep in your own room tonight."

"Ruby."

"I'm sorry" is the last thing she says before she walks out of the room.

I knew this conversation wasn't going to go well, but I didn't think it would crush me or be the end of us.

I blow out a breath.

How are we going to tell the kids?

Fuck.

There is no we.

Not anymore.

CHAPTER TWENTY-SEVEN

RUBY

As soon as I woke up, I told Max we were spending the day at the beach.

So that's where we are.

I'd also sent Shay a text to meet me here, giving her only a summed-up version of what happened.

I thought about texting Grace or Brooke, but I needed someone who has known me longer and better.

I need someone who knew me back when I was living with Colt.

My relationship with Shay is different from my brothers' spouses. Shay went to the same college I did before she moved back to Lovers. We'd find time to meet between classes and become good friends.

But by the time I'd moved back last summer, she and Luca had their own thing going, and he sucked up all her time.

I don't blame her for picking him over me, but right now, I could really use one of my closest friends.

Max is running across the beach with a soccer ball by the time Shay lowers herself to sit next to me in the sand.

She lets out a breath.

"Declan's really going to leave?" she asks.

Word travels fast in a small town.

"Yeah, he is."

"You can't make it work?"

"He thinks we can, but you know how it goes with long distance and there are kids involved. Maybe if it was just me …"

I'd thought about it a lot last night after Declan finally made his way to his room.

Would my choice be different if it were just me?

Had I not uprooted my life once before for someone, would I be saying yes?

If I weren't so worried about what people would say about me following another man out of town, would I have said yes?

"I think I'm broken," I say quietly.

"Why do you think that?"

"Because my heart hurts and I want him to stay, but I could never live with myself if he gave up anything in his life to stay with me. Here. To pick me. Like, what makes me so important that he should change all his goals in life for me?"

Shay blows out a breath. "That one is tricky. I think it's different because you love him."

I do.

"I'm going to miss him so much," I say and then suck in a breath to keep myself from crying. "Max is going to miss Susie, too, and I just don't want to be sad again. I don't want to *feel* broken again. Like I still wasn't good enough for someone."

The crazy part is that he was about to pick me. He was about to say he'd stay. I could have just let him, and he would have never known about the offer from Colt's dad. But I couldn't let him pick me.

And that's what makes me feel broken. I had everything I wanted right then, and I didn't take it.

Silence settles over us, and then I hear her sniffle.

Her color is off and she looks tired.

Is she that worried about me?

"Hey," I say and scoot closer to her. "Don't cry. I cried enough for both of us last night, alright?"

She nods and then blurts out, "I'm pregnant."

I gasp.

"What?"

"Yeah, like super fucking pregnant."

"Shay! That's wonderful." I wrap my arms around her as she begins to sob.

"No, no, why are we crying?"

I try to wipe her tears away, but it's no use.

"Because you're sitting here heartbroken and I'm … stupid happy right now."

I stick my bottom lip out and my eyes well with tears to match hers.

"And we are going to be extra stupid happy for a long, long time together."

She burst into tears again.

"And I've been sick a lot. I can't eat, but I just want cookie dough, and I … I want to make this all better for you and I can't, and *everything* makes me cry."

I let out a small laugh while sniffling right along with her.

"You're making me an aunt—you've already made my day better."

"I think I made it worse."

"Nope. You did not. I choose to be happy for the rest of the day because of this news."

She leans into me, and I hug her tight.

I'll go back to being sad when I'm alone.

"Hey, Ruby?"

"Yeah?

"You know how you said that you'd never forgive yourself if you let him give up his goals?"

"Yes," I say and attempt to clean my tear-stricken face.

"Well, I think you're forgetting something very important about all that."

"What?"

"What if being with you was one of his goals?"

And just like that, I start crying all over again.

"The things we want in life change when we change, Ruby. It's just a matter of how you accept that change and what you're going to do about it."

I let her words sink in as we sit there hugging in the sand.

She's right.

The past few months have changed me in more ways than I ever knew possible.

Now, I just need to decide which direction to go with it.

CHAPTER TWENTY-EIGHT

DECLAN

Just two days ago, I was asking my girlfriend to move in with me, and now I'm moving to a different state with no girlfriend.

It doesn't even feel like my life right now.

I plan to return to Lovers, but at this point, I don't know if it's for good or to sell my house.

I hope it's the former, but I have to find a way to fix my company first, and right now, I just don't know how I can do that without putting in the time back in Chicago.

Miles, Luca, and Hudson put together a little going away lunch shindig for me at Miles's house. It's weird to have everyone together here instead of at Ruby's. It's even weirder that they all know I'm the reason Ruby isn't here and not a single one of them has tried to punch me.

"Do you leave right after this?" Shay asks, and I nod, my gaze outside the kitchen window where the kids are sitting on Miles's tire swing. It's not moving, and there isn't a smile in sight.

"How's Susie doing?"

I sigh and then turn, leaning onto the counter. "She's not

talking to me. I know she can hear me, because she does the things I ask of her, but she is mad. Rightfully so. Max, too."

Shay rubs my arm.

"It's going to work out eventually."

She forces a smile.

"I know that's the last thing you want to hear, but it's true. I can't tell you when it will happen, but if you two are truly meant to be together, which I think you are, you'll find a way back to each other."

I don't reply, because what am I supposed to say? I know I could change all this by not leaving and giving up my company.

I just don't know if I can do it.

We eat, and the mood is down. The kids don't even play. They just sit at the table with the rest of us.

My gaze drifts to the empty spot next to Max, whom Luca picked up on his way here.

Ruby isn't here.

Still, once the dishes are done and everyone is preparing to say their goodbyes, I turn to her brothers and say the obvious. "She's not coming, is she?"

They exchange a few looks, and then Miles shakes his head.

"I'm sorry, Dec, she's not."

I nod slowly and then look out over the yard.

This is her life. Her friends. Her family.

And I'm the reason she isn't here.

I'm not going to say it might be for the best that I'm leaving, because nothing is best if it doesn't include Ruby, but I …

I'm doing this to myself. The simple answer is to just say *fuck it*. Fuck the company I built and the people who work there and lose it all so I can be with Ruby.

But it's not that simple.

"She's …" Hudson starts but never finishes.

"Hurt, but it's weird," Miles says, clearly having no problem with his words. "She thinks you're doing the right thing. And I don't get it."

"Neither do I," Luca says. "The right thing is you staying in Lovers with her and figuring this shit out with your company while you're here."

"If that were an option for me, I would take it."

"You own the company, make it an option," Luca suggests, as if it were that simple.

I look at him and sigh. His shoulders drop.

"I know. I know."

Paul comes over and hugs me goodbye and then wraps Susie in a bear hug, swaying her back and forth. Then the rest of the Ashers take their turn, followed by Quinn, Sadie, and Shay.

"See you at the wedding," I tell Hudson and Sadie, and then I hug Shay. "Congratulations, Shay, you're going to be a wonderful mom."

"Thank you."

I clear my throat because I'm dreading the next part, yet there's no way to avoid it.

"Come on, Susie, we need to get on the road to catch our flight."

That's when the tears hit and my heart breaks.

"I don't want to go," she says quietly.

"I know, hunny. Neither do I." I squat down to her level.

Max is standing next to her, and although he isn't crying, the look on his face is about to break me even more.

"I don't want you to leave either," he admits and then wraps his arms around my neck. "And I know my mom doesn't either, even if she's not here."

I pat his back, refusing to let them see me cry.

"I love you, you know that, right? And I will always love your mom."

He nods. But when he and Susie hug, I have to look away.

Shay's and Sadie's tears make me feel even more like shit.

Susie puts her hand in mine and waves one more goodbye as we walk out the door.

"I wish it wasn't on you alone to save your company, Dad. I wish you had someone who could do it for you so that we can stay."

I pick her up and hold her close the rest of the way to my truck.

As soon as I pull away, I glance at my daughter in the rearview mirror. She's staring at a picture in her hand.

"What's that?" I ask.

"A picture of me and Max."

"Can I see it?"

I reach back as she hands it to me.

But my eyes don't go to the kids in the center—they go to the man in the back who is clearly photobombing the kids.

Colter fucking Davenport.

The way he does business is wild to me.

Colter's words from that night on the patio ring through my mind. If he doesn't like the way his dad does business, maybe he'd like to work with me instead.

There's only one way to find out.

CHAPTER TWENTY-NINE

RUBY

The next Sunday breakfast comes around all too fast, and my mind is struggling to accept that just a little over a week ago Declan told me he was leaving, and by today, there isn't anything left in this house to remember him.

"Hey, are you coming outside to eat?" Sadie asks, poking her head through the sliding door.

I shake my head, as if that can clear the thoughts. "Yes. Sorry."

She smiles sweetly. "It's okay."

I follow her out and take a seat.

Everyone has their food plated, but not a single person has taken a bite.

"Were you waiting for me?"

"Yes," Luca says.

Miles punches his arm.

"What? You're worried, too. Stop acting like you're not. Why aren't we bombarding her like you did me?"

"I'm fine," I say quickly and then dish up my own plate. I even take a giant bite to drive the point home.

With my fork, I point at Max's plate. "Eat, please."

"No," he clips back quickly and with a fire I've never heard from him before. In fact, the entire table is shocked. Every single head turns to look at my son.

I don't even have it in me to scold him, because I know where this tone is coming from.

Instead, I point to his plate again.

"You need to eat."

"I'm not eating." He stands abruptly and storms inside.

My dad scoots his chair back, but I put my hand on his arm. "Don't. It's fine."

"It's not fine. He knows better."

"He's hurt. I'm his mother. I'm allowing it right now. I'll talk to him in a bit."

Dad studies me for a moment and then nods.

"Now, can we all just eat?"

As soon as they all begin, I finally say what has been on my mind since the day Declan left.

"Did I make a mistake?"

My mind has raced over this day after day. Even more so when Barton caught wind that I didn't do what he asked. He was quick to send me an updated balance.

Looking at the setback only made me more confident in my decision to tell Declan to go.

But fuck, my heart hurts so much.

Awkward glances are exchanged around the table.

No one replies.

"Should I have gone with him?"

Declan staying was never going to be an option, but Max and I not going with him, that's all on me.

"Do you think you should have?" Quinn asks.

I shrug.

"I don't know. I'm just numb, and nothing feels right here

without them."

My eyes sting.

"I miss him, and it's only been a week."

Crying in front of my entire family wasn't on my bingo card at any point in my life, but here I am, doing it anyway.

My dad is the first to stand and hug me. "Oh, Ruby, if it feels wrong to be here without them, why didn't you go?"

"Because that would mean I'm leaving this place again for another guy. The rumors were bad enough before; I can only imagine what they would be like this time."

To my surprise, Miles laughs.

Quinn elbows him. "Stop."

"I'm sorry." He holds up his hands. "It's not funny. None of this is funny. It's just that I hate to break it to you, Ruby, but you're an Asher. We all found a way to self-sabotage ourselves over the person we love, and this is your turn."

"And that's funny because?"

"Because this is also the moment where you figure it out."

I huff.

"But I'm not. I'm confused and scared and—"

"Do you love him?" Hudson asks.

I nod. "Like a stupid amount."

"And you want to be with him?" Luca asks.

"Yes."

"And do you truly care what anyone thinks?" Miles asks.

"I …"

It's a question I've asked myself many times, but for some reason, sitting here with my family, it processes differently in my mind.

No, I don't care what the town thinks. I care about how the rumors affect my family.

"I care that you all have to walk around town and hear what

people think of me, and I feel like when I make bad choices, I let you down."

"Let us down? How in the hell do you do that?" Hudson asks, and I can see in his eyes that it's a genuine question.

"Everyone thinks I left to follow Colt because his—"

"We know why you left," my dad cuts in. "Look at the life you have given Max. It's incredible the choice you made."

"What?"

"You're the most selfless person we know, Ruby," Miles adds. "These people can say anything they want, but we don't listen. They don't know you."

"Yeah, it's a little intimidating how awesome you are." Luca grins.

"Let's not forget that you do it all on your own as a fucking mom. It's impressive as shit, Ruby."

I have no words.

They're proud of me? But they never say anything.

I sit there for another second, no doubt with shock written all over my face.

"Well, it's about time you all said something." Sadie nudges Hudson.

"And you better do more of it from here on out," Quinn says, grabbing another piece of bacon.

"I …" is all Shay gets out through her tears.

"I'm sorry if we ever made you doubt how proud we are of you, Ruby," my dad says and stands to hug me where I sit. "But the question remains: why are you still here? Declan isn't just some guy, and he sure as hell isn't going to steal you away from us for years on end. You'll be back more than enough with that one. And here or there, wherever you end up, we are still going to think nothing but the best of you."

"But …"

"Go get them, Mom," Max says from the doorway. "I miss them, too."

I wipe the tears off my cheek and share a look with everyone at the table. Of course, I start crying again when I make eye contact with Shay, because she's crying even harder now.

"Are you all okay watching Max until I get back?"

"What?" Max squeaks behind me. "I'm coming, too."

He earns a laugh from everyone for that one, but it only lasts a moment before everyone gets to work. An hour later, Max and I are in the car headed for the airport in Wind Valley.

———

BY THE TIME the wheels touch down in Chicago, my confidence has slipped a little.

We both practically run to the area where an Uber will pick us up, wheeling carry-on bags behind us, and take us to Declan's offices.

"Are you nervous?" Max asks, his focus on my bouncing knee.

"A little."

"Don't be. He told me how much he loved you the day he left."

I fight back the tears.

I never let Declan say the words that night, but it seems he was going to make sure I knew them either way.

I just hope I'm not too late.

The car pulls to a stop outside his building, and Max's eyes go wide.

"He owns this?"

"Not all of it, just a few floors."

With Max's hand in mine, we march into the building.

I check in with security, and they direct us to the elevators.

Max and I don't speak as we take it all in, but that's okay. I think the silence speaks volumes for both of us.

The elevator doors open to Declan's floor, and the hustle and bustle of a business is in full force. Yet, to the right, Susie is sitting in her own cubicle, watching a movie.

She glances up, then looks back to her iPad, and then back up.

She jerks her headphones over her head and drops the tablet to the desk, running to us with a high-pitched squeal and leaping into my arms.

"I missed you!" she says.

"We missed you, too," I tell her and then set her down. She and Max immediately pick up where they left off, Max rescuing her iPad and sharing the chair.

Okay, well, I'm on my own now.

"Susie, why are you …" Declan's words are cut short when he sees Max, his head immediately jerking to the entrance where I'm standing.

My heart slams into my chest, and for the first time in days, I feel like I can finally breathe again.

All by just seeing him.

It's him, but different. He's not in his day-to-day sweats and T-shirt. He's in a suit and tie, and he looks really good.

Because I don't know what to do and we clearly now have an audience, I wave.

His stunned expression changes to fighting a smile.

He waves back.

I step toward him.

I had a whole speech planned, but the moment we are toe to toe and he looks into my eyes, I simply speak from the heart.

"I miss you," I whisper and then hold my chin high.

He doesn't reply.

I swipe away a tear and then sniffle. Nothing about this is

pretty, but I won't give up. "Every day. And I don't care where it is, I just want to be where you are. I know I said all that stuff about not repeating my past, but this is different. *We* are different. This is my *future*. I need you in my life. Max and I need you and Susie."

I pause, waiting for Declan to move, flinch, or say something. He only stares at me with a look of disbelief in his eyes.

"I know what I said back in Lovers. I—"

"Alright, it's ready. I just had to have … oh shit."

Colt steps out of an office.

My heart immediately sinks as I look back and forth between them. Are they working together now? Why else would Colt be here? If they are working together, does that mean Declan is working with Barton?

"I have to go."

"Wait," Declan says.

"I …" I spin around and point at Colt. "I texted you hours ago and told you Max and I were headed to Chicago, but you never said you were here."

"You knew she was coming?" Declan asks him.

"I did, and yes, but I wasn't going to ruin this."

"Too late," I say "Max, we're leaving."

"Ruby, hold on a second," Declan says again.

I don't listen. I start jamming my finger on the elevator button. "Come on. Come on."

"Ruby."

I drop my chin to my chest as Declan's voice surrounds me.

Just once, once, I'd like something to work out in my favor.

The simple thought makes me want to cry all over again.

"It's okay Dec. You don't have to say anything."

I wipe at my cheeks to save some kind of dignity, then turn to look at him.

"You're just doing what's best for you and Susie. I know." I look at Colt. "Please bring Max down in five minutes."

He nods.

The elevator doors open and I step in. I press the "L" button and wait, arms crossed and gaze down as I wait for the doors to close, knowing Declan is going to stare at me until they do.

For what? What reason would he have to just watch me fall apart?

I close my eyes for the last few seconds, and then finally breathe a sigh of relief when the doors close.

"Oh God," I say and let the tears break.

"Baby, please don't cry," Declan says from beside me.

I startle and then I can't help it. I break down.

"Instead of giving a speech on everything I'm thinking I'll get right to the point," he says. He steps in front of me, his finger under my chin, gently forcing me to look at him. "What's best for me and Susie is being wherever you and Max are."

"What?"

"I sold the company to Colt."

Oh my God.

"You what? But Declan, that wasn't your goal. That wasn't what you wanted. All that stuff with Susie's mom and what you need to—"

"Baby, I'm miserable without you, and I don't need this company. I need you. I know I've made mistakes before, but those choices have led me to you, and letting you go was not a mistake I was going to make. Not again."

"But you love this place."

"I love you more."

"You do?"

He nods.

"I love you so damn much, Ruby Asher, and as soon as this deal is done, I'm coming back to Lovers. For good."

"You are?" I ask, even though it's silly because he clearly just said so.

"I am." He steps closer, backing me up against the elevator wall. "And I know I don't deserve it, but I want us to pick back up where we were. With you and Max moving in with me and Susie, all of us doing this family thing forever."

I chuckle through happy tears. God, I'm a mess. "Is that a proposal?"

He shakes his head.

"I am going to marry you someday, but when I propose, you won't have to question whether I am or not. Got it?"

I bite my lips.

"Got it."

He swoops me into his arms and kisses me as if his life depends on it.

And I will choose to let him kiss every single day for the rest of our lives.

EPILOGUE

RUBY

Hudson cried during the ceremony, and I won a hundred bucks from Miles, Luca, and my dad.

They misjudged him, but not me.

Sadie had shared enough during our girls' nights and his opinions on this day—I knew my brother was going to shed at least one tear.

What I didn't expect was for it to be the moment the doors opened and Sadie appeared. I thought he'd at least wait until they were holding hands at the altar.

"What are you going to do with your money?" Declan asks, handing me a glass of wine.

I smirk and then pull the money from where I'd tucked it into my bralette. My maid of honor dress doesn't have pockets, so I had to improvise.

"I'm not sure yet. Maybe take you and the kids to a fancy dinner."

"I would never let you pay for that."

"You can and you will if it's what I want."

He chuckles.

"You're not wrong about that." He slinks his free hand around my body, pulling me in for a kiss. "I live to make you happy."

"Same."

His lips meet mine, and I melt into him.

Kissing Declan never gets old.

His hand smooths over the back of my dress, falling dangerously close to my butt.

I laugh into the kiss, and he pulls away.

A throat clears next to us, and Sandy, from the kids' school, glares at us just before she leans into Cami and starts talking.

"New rumor alert," Declan whispers into my ear.

I kiss him again, slipping some tongue for dramatics.

"Let them talk."

After I left Chicago, Max and I were home for no more than a week before Declan and Susie were back.

A couple of weeks after that, we were all moving into Declan's house, and now the wedding of the summer is finally here.

Then Declan found out about the deal Barton offered me. It wasn't like I tried to hide it, but I didn't think it was something that needed to be discussed, since there was nothing we could do about it.

Except that when I refused to take money from Declan, he contacted everyone—and I mean everyone—that he knows and told them to consider working with me. Then he called Colt, who did the same.

Needless to say that if work continues the way it is, I'll have that loan and the stupid interest added paid off in less than a year.

If you had asked me at the start of this summer if I thought

I'd fall madly in love with Declan Young and watch him become friends with Max's father, I would have laughed.

But it turns out, Declan and Susie were the missing pieces that my crazy family needed.

"Okay, okay, we get it," Linc says, pulling up a chair at the table right behind us. "You're in love, too. No need to show it off in front of all of us."

Declan and I pull apart, still lacing our hands, and I frown at Linc.

"That dating app isn't working out, huh?"

He grunts.

"I know there are single women in Lovers, but none of them interest me, and the two I met in Wind Valley weren't ... we didn't jive."

"Probably because you said *jive*," I say and Declan laughs. "Is that an older man thing?"

Linc points a finger at me. "Declan isn't that much younger than me, Ruby."

"She wasn't talking about me," Declan adds.

Linc just sighs. "It's not as easy as I thought it would be."

I reach out and rub his shoulder. "Love comes when you least expect it. At least it did for me."

He nods. "That's the thing though. I feel like I have to have some dramatic backstory to my life that I'm trying to overcome to find love. All the great love stories have it, but what about us average Joes, huh? We deserve a love story, too, even though our lives are good, happy. We just want someone to share it with."

I stick out my bottom lip. I want that for him, too.

"No woman wants a man who has his shit together and is confident with the direction his life is going. They want the man who needs to be fixed just as much as they want to fix themselves. I think I'm doomed," he adds and then gets up to leave.

"I hope he finds someone someday," I say, snuggling in

under Declan's arm. "I mean, look at you. You don't have some elaborate backstory, and you found love."

"Yeah, with the woman who lived next door and hated me because I'm just so damn cool and smart and the town favorite."

I roll my eyes. "Who is Linc's enemy? Maybe that's the direction he needs to go."

Declan rubs his chin.

"Ah, yeah, well, I think Linc is too nice to have enemies."

"Bummer. I'll have to keep thinking. It must be something about weddings and all the love in the air," I say with a laugh.

A slow song comes on, and Declan pulls me onto the dance floor.

"If we want to keep up this chat about couples,"—Declan nods to the side of the room—"tell me about that." He points to where Gavin Richford and Brooke are standing in the corner.

I smile. "That's Gavin."

Declan pinches my side playfully.

"I know who he is. Dutton has been trying to recruit him to the basketball team. But he seems to be standing pretty close to Brooke."

"Oh, yeah, that's nothing. Brooke has zero interest in the Richford family."

"Except when it comes to Grace."

"Of course, since she's her friend."

"The Richfords just have the two boys and the two girls, right? I interact with Dutton mostly, and Grace when the group is together, but the others, I've never really spoken to."

I nod.

"Yep, Dutton, Grace, Gavin, and Wren, but Wren doesn't live here. She's still away at college, living in an off-campus apartment, so she hardly even comes home in the summer."

"And are the others all part of the lodge here?"

"Do you really not know the answers to these questions? You did grow up here."

"I probably should, but I don't ask that many when it's just us guys. And as you know, I was a little too busy being the best at everything to be social."

Again, I roll my eyes, but this time he kisses me.

"You should know these things. You're officially a small-town guy again."

"Just fill me in."

"Okay, so Dutton is the oldest, and he was always in trouble growing up. He had that real bad boy image going for him during high school, but he left for college and moved back after he graduated. Classic small-town boy move."

"I knew that much, Ruby."

"Fine. Then there is Grace. She also did the college thing but doubled up on classes to come back and run the Lodge. Did you know their dad is about to retire and he's going to have to pick between Grace and Dutton?"

"Is Grace as competitive as Dutton?"

"Very. Then there is Gavin, who I'm surprised is here, because he's a single dad and goes nowhere without his daughter. Then there is Wren—she was an oopsie baby."

"How do you know all of this?" Declan asks.

"I like to ask questions," I answer with a shrug. "Girls' nights are never short of discussion."

"Do you think people ask these kinds of questions about us?"

I volley my head. "Probably."

The song changes to something faster, and the kids run out to us on the dance floor. Susie immediately goes to dance with Declan and Max with me. The bride and groom take a spot next to us, and then Miles, Quinn, Luca, Shay, and my dad appear.

Soon, all our friends are on the floor, and everyone is dancing and singing to the words.

Declan's eyes catch mine over the kids, and he mouths, *I love you.*

I love you, too, I mouth back and then can't help but smile.

This is my life now, and I wouldn't trade it for anything in the world.

Keep reading for a bonus epilogue for Declan and Ruby.

BONUS EPILOGUE

RUBY - THREE YEARS LATER

No matter how many times I dreamt of this day, not a single one of them compares to how magical it actually turned out.

Right now, my father is holding his arms out for me, and in a matter of minutes, Declan Young will officially be my husband.

Three years ago, when I invited him to move into my basement, all because I didn't want to make my son sad, I had no idea how much my life was going to change.

I had no idea I was going to meet the love of my life, who brought me a daughter.

I had no idea just how beautiful each day could be.

I try not to let the emotions of the day get to me, and I step toward my dad and loop my arms with his. We turn, facing the small group of friends and family who are standing to watch me walk down the aisle. My gaze only focuses on them for the smallest of moments before my attention is stolen by the man at the end of this walk.

Declan Young.

Just behind him is Max, followed by all three of my brothers.

Susie stands at the front of the girls' side, with Sadie, Quinn, and Shay behind her.

Can't Help Falling In Love by Kina Grannis begins to play, and I take my first step.

Declan holds my gaze the entire time, and the smile on my face only grows.

He takes my hands when I reach him, and my heart flutters the same way it did the first time he kissed me.

Hi, he mouths and then winks at me. His eyes slowly take me in, and with a room full of people, it feels as if he's undressing me.

When his gaze reaches mine again, I mouth back, *stop*.

The grin he gives me and the dark look in his eyes remain on me until we hear the words I've been waiting to hear since the day he proposed to me.

"I now pronounce you husband and wife."

The crowd cheers, and Declan kisses me as if no one is watching.

And right now, I wish they weren't.

***

"Does she have any idea?" I ask, watching as Susie and Max run around the room, playing with their cousins or friends. The evening has been filled with dancing and food and fun all night long, but right now, Declan and I are sitting at our little table for two, finally getting to eat.

Thank goodness the kitchen at Lover Lodge made separate plates for us and included time for the bride and groom to eat during the schedule of the evening.

I am famished.

I scoop some mac n cheese onto my spoon and eat it as if I haven't eaten all day. Which I have, many times.

It's hard to skip a meal when you're eating for two.

A secret that I've yet to share with anyone, including Declan. I have a surprise planned for him when we get home for the night.

The kids are staying at the lodge with Declan's parents and Colt.

Max's father splurged for a suite that has multiple rooms so the kids could make a fort in the living room, while he and the grandparents still have their own spaces.

"No, I don't think she does, but she's going to be over the moon when we tell her."

My eyes find Susie, and the tears begin as if they have their own mind.

I'm furious that Susie's mother signed over her parental rights with no questions asked, but I'm also overwhelmed with a newfound happiness that soon Susie will officially be my daughter. I considered her such without the legality of it all, but this, this moment is huge for me. Her. Us.

Add in a baby, and my life is nothing short of perfect.

A screaming baby steals my attention to another part of the room, and I welcome the distraction. We still have a couple of hours left to go, and I don't want to ruin my makeup for photos.

The screaming is followed quickly by laughter as Colt and my brothers all seem to be on the verge of a dance off, Susie and Max now joining Colt's team.

Colt and Declan, since day one, have hit it off, and even though I wasn't sure how I felt about it at first, I love the fact that they are friends now. One might even call them best friends at this point. They talk all the time and have even teamed to plan more than one family vacation.

We've gone on many just us four, but we don't hate it when Colt is around. Alone time with Declan is a lot easier when there is another adult around. I know how lucky I am to have a family that blends well together.

Now, if only we could find the right woman for Colt.

I'm elated for the love I found, but I can't wait for the day he finds it, too.

I choke up instantly at my own thoughts, and the tears reappear.

"Baby, what's wrong?" Decans asks, abandoning his steak and turning to face me, and gives me all his attention.

"Nothing," I say quickly and shrug it off, but I know better. Decaln isn't going to just let the fact that his *wife* his sitting here crying go.

"He threads his fingers with mine and gently reaches for my chin, guiding me to look at him.

"What is it?"

My bottom lip shakes, and even though I have a surprise later, I can't keep it in.

"I'm pregnant," I tell him, and he freezes.

I swear it feels like an eternity waiting for him to react, but it's worth it.

"Are you serious?" His entire face lights up, and his eyes start to gloss over.

I nod.

His hand unlaces from mine to cover my stomach, and then his lips are on mine again.

He pulls back.

"We're having a baby?"

I nod, and he kisses me again, letting the tears fall freely now because his happiness has set them off again.

When he breaks the kiss again, his hand comes to my face to brush the wetness away.

"I love you with all my heart, Ruby Asher."

I cup his face and rest my forehead on his, "It's Ruby Young now, and I love you, too."

*****

Don't miss out on news of the next series by Jami Rogers. The series title and characters will be revealed in the coming months, but will be shared in her newsletter first.
Join Jami's mailing list here.

MORE BOOKS BY JAMI ROGERS

For the full list of titles by Jami Rogers, please visit www. authorjamirogers.com.

Or scan the QR code below.

FOLLOW JAMI

Want more from Jami?

Join Jami's mailing list for exclusive bonus epilogues,
giveaways, and all the book news!

Visit her website
www.authorjamirogers.com

Or join her Facebook group
Jami Rogers Readers

facebook.com/AuthorJamiRogers

instagram.com/authorjamirogers

bookbub.com/authors/authorjamirogers

goodreads.com/jamirogers

tiktok.com/@authorjamirogers

ABOUT THE AUTHOR

My name is Jami Rogers and I write fun, fast, and flirty slow-burn contemporary romance novels with heat. I *love* love and want to share my passion for happily ever afters with the world.

I was born in Wyoming and still live in the cowboy state with my husband, daughter, and fur babies. I like to read, write, run, watch movies/TV, and spend time with my family. I'm horrible at returning phone calls and prefer to text, but I still struggle to hit the little blue arrow to send a message once I'm finished typing my reply. My husband does 90% of the cooking in our house. Not because I'm busy – I'm just simply a lousy cook.

facebook.com/AuthorJamiRogers

instagram.com/authorjamirogers

goodreads.com/jamirogers

bookbub.com/profile/jami-rogers

tiktok.com/@authorjamirogers

www.ingramcontent.com/pod-product-compliance
Lightning Source LLC
Chambersburg PA
CBHW032358310726

48973CB00007B/2068